SEAN MILLER

a novel by

JOHN FRANCIS

SILVERDART
MMVIII

Published by Silverdart Ltd
211 Linton House, 164-180 Union Street
London SE1 0LH, United Kingdom
www.silverdart.co.uk
Tel: +44 (0) 20 7928 7770
enquiries@silverdart.co.uk

Part of the proceeds of this book go to
The Cirencester Stroke Club

Copyright © 2008 John Francis

All rights reserved. No part of this publication may be reproduced,
stored in a retrieval system, or transmitted, in any form or by any means,
electronic, mechanical, photocopying, recording or otherwise, without the
prior permission of the publisher and the copyright owner.

Printed and bound by
Biddles Ltd, King's Lynn, Norfolk

ISBN-13   978-0-9554581-1-8 (Hardback)
ISBN-13   978-0-9554581-2-5 (Paperback)

ILLUSTRATIONS

Cover: images of two paintings have been used to create this illustration –
'The Defence at the Battle of the First of June 1794'
by Nicholas Pocock (1811), photo © The National Maritime Museum,
London, Greenwich Hospital Collection; and
'A Girl' by a follower of Jean-Baptiste Greuze,
late 18th century, photo © The National Gallery.
Both images are reproduced with kind permission.

The illustration on page 202 is by John Francis

This book is dedicated to
Anne Francis,
my wife, carer and
competent seawoman.

A glossary of nautical terms is included on pages 195 to 199.

The lines of battle of the British and French fleets in the Battle of 1st June, 1794 are shown on page 200 and 201.

Information about the author is on page 203.

Acknowledgements are given on page 204.

ANDREW MILLER'S PREFACE

I never heard it philosophically asserted that one misfortune in life should have counter-balance in an equal and opposite stroke of good fortune. Yet the month of November in the year 1790 saw just such a turn of fate occur to me, and on successive days too.

Here follows an earnest account of my memoirs, the story of a country lad turned seaman in good King George's navy. As I take pen, the passion leading to my flight from my village of Broadwell is still impressed upon my mind. So also are the chiefest events that were about to afflict England, commencing in the year 1793, and the persons of my shipmates from admiral and captain to the humblest of my messmates of the gundecks.

However I cannot say the same of the clashes of great emperors on the shore. Their doings lay beyond the wit of a mere seaman boy, and I have therefore had recourse to the journals of the period, to my imagination and my memory, and to the log I kept of my own doings in the Great War. Alas, I fear its accuracy cannot be sworn to, so I must crave the reader's indulgence.

For those untutored in the sailors' tongue, I have prepared a Glossary of Nautical Terms, on pages 195 to 199.

I offer you this tale as a means to learn about the extraordinary times that I had the fortune to live through.

A.M.
In the year of our Lord 1830.

GREAT BRITAIN

Plymouth • • Portsmouth
Prawle Point

Battle of 1st June 1794 L'Aberwrac'h
Ushant •
Brest

FRANCE

BISCAY

Cabo Finisterra •

Toulon •

SPAIN

Gibraltar •

NORTH AFRICA

PART 1 – PORTSMOUTH TOWN

CHAPTER 1

First, I must introduce myself to the esteemed reader.

I was named Andrew Miller, the son of one Jack Miller, a sailor in the English fleet who was lost at sea before I was born. At least that is what my mother told me. To give me birth she had removed to her aunt's place, a flour mill in the county of Hampshire, since her own mother was in poor health and not able to attend her. Then, while I was still at a tender age, she returned to her father's home in the village of Broadwell, which lies on the edge of Dorset.

We had residence in an establishment of a better sort than the usual run of country public houses. Its signboard was emblazoned 'The Benbow's Head', and there I grew to help around the taproom and the smallholding which adjoined the inn. From our position on a crossroads and a coaching stage, we attracted a deal of trade from travellers and locals, including the gentry. My life was full of incident then.

It must be confessed that my mother was also a centre for this attraction and gossip, indeed the main one, causing me endless embarrassment and raillery amongst my fellows.

I learnt that, as a young girl, she had been schooled at an academy for young ladies where the teachers of French outnumbered those of English, and the teachers of the three 'Ds' – deportment, dance and dress – outnumbered everything. She had been the belle of most hunt balls and the toast of the hunting set throughout the county.

As I grew up, the 'widow Miller', as she was then commonly called, was a comely and well-spoken beauty, who was taking charge of the entertaining as my grandmother declined. Soon her kitchen became famous round and about.

As I grew older I recognised those who were suitors for her hand, but they got naught but the gentlest of rejections. Grandfather became more and more the farmer, and less and less the landlord, with me as his helper – a country lad.

Nine or ten boys became scholars when the new curate's lady opened a class in writing and numbering, and I took to the penny lessons with the best of them, always, however, agog for the schooling to end and the night's poaching to begin in season.

I was aged sixteen summers, when I first had doubts of mother's intentions. I now see that her aloof ways had changed abruptly when Sir John Blunder, who was the squire, came to sup at the Benbow. Sir John brought with him his elder son, Richard, whom he had sent to Oxford an age before and was returned at the age of thirty-four to live at Broadwell. Richard was now a Bachelor by degree and a dandy by inclination.

Apparently plans had been laid beforehand for a supper of some pretensions, at which mother was to sit at the table of the squire and his son as their hostess. The dining room gleamed with extra candelabra and glassware. For the occasion she appeared in a shimmering white gown of the new fashion, which allowed the feet to be glimpsed, clad in silken shoes and laced round the ankles. There were whisperings and gasps of admiration from the surrounding tables which accommodated the gentry and their ladies.

Even a raw youth could recognise the interplay of meaning looks that ensued, though their import escaped me at first. The squire introduced my mother, who was only some two years' younger than Richard, by her given name, Janine, adding 'the widow Miller.' He took mother's hand to his lips, squinting all the time at his son's expression. I saw Richard's stiff, blank eyes fix on mother, a slow flush spreading over his face, and he looked quickly away, unsure whether to kiss her hand or not, and annoyed at his lack of decision.

The squire was not finished yet. Catching sight of me, he pulled me into the circle and, staring from his son to me and back, loudly spoke my name. I was struck aback to determine his purpose, although he was known for his eccentricities. It was as if mother had expected this pass to come about, for she kept a straight face and appeared unconcerned, indeed rather detached, as one possessed of a secret. The squire resumed his normal jollity and the incident seemed to be over, as the dinner advanced.

I came and went, however, serving and collecting ale mugs in snug and taproom, and occasionally passing into the dining room. I sensed the younger Blunder forever staring at me, while my mother had no eyes for anyone but that handsome young man himself. I was much disturbed.

On the days thereafter, I came often upon Richard Blunder and mother locked in tight conversation, and the young blade began to frequent the inn night and day. Despite the new sparkle that had lighted her countenance on his first arrival, she now appeared troubled and tense whenever I came into her company.

Matters continued thus for some time, becoming more difficult to my troubled mind. However they came to a head one November night, when the village boys and I were returning from Lord Seckberg's copses – Seckberg being a wealthy landowner in those parts.

We were laden with nets, traps and other paraphernalia

of the poacher, but our bag had been small and we were in disgruntled mood. This came to an end however, when a dark figure rounded the corner towards our barn.

A whisper of 'Mister Richard' came to my ears, followed by youthful sniggers. "Watch him Miller, you'll be Lord o' the Manor if'n he gets 'is way!" They dissolved in suppressed laughter.

In the barn, voices flared out in anger. Following inside, I found Richard Blunder was clasping mother tightly in his arms. She was flushed scarlet and Blunder hissing in high passion.

"I tell you, for my child to inherit there must be no prior entanglement; there is no room here for Andrew, though he may be a bastard of mine," he snarled.

Like a thunderclap it burst upon me that I was the subject of their dispute. So here was my true father – no bold sailor, but an idle landowner-to-be. Everyone but me had seen our likeness.

My mother was adamant. "I'll not send him to Morris's, they'll starve him to death. So there shall be no thought of a marrying, I swear it".

A catch came in my mother's throat, and she shrieked, "I absolve you from your second bastard, Richard Blunder, as you disown the first. Go, you pig, go, or it will soon become obvious who has fathered my shame."

In a flood of tears, she caressed her belly absently.

Blunder roared that they should wed, by God, and he babbled drunkenly that his father would not stomach two by-blows. The new one would be born in wedlock, as planned.

My brain stumbled over these new revelations. Was my mother with child – a wedding planned? That Blunder would get rid of me was patently obvious. Nothing could be easier in those days, I knew. Now that farms were being enclosed fast and fewer hands employed, there were hiring fairs to contract a youngster to the back-hills farms.

A trivial wage was paid for the labour of a year or two, but most were worked to death or suffered starvation, like those gaol prisoners, who are sentenced to slavery in the Americas. The poorer village boys feared the hiring fairs more than gaol itself.

Richard Blunder was foaming and stamping like a mad bull. Suddenly he flung mother to the ground and she screamed as she fell, clutching herself. Bunder leapt upon her to receive a shower of scratches on his face as they fought in the loose hay. She lay, pleading beneath his plunging body, her legs all bared.

I sprang forward in a rage – neither had seen me.

He seemed to sober when I pulled him roughly from my mother's sobbing form. I aimed kicks at his legs as he scrambled from the flagstones drawing a cudgel from his coat like a common footpad. My beating began then and, apart from the shadow of his arm rising and falling, I remembered no more until the early dawn.

The lantern was still alight in the barn and I heard a soft murmuring in the sheaves of straw. It came from my mother who lay caressing her lover, not seeing or hearing aught else in her torrent of kissing. She was whispering reassurances he should have his way and that I should be banished from Broadwell.

I knew then that he had cozened her out of her previous resolve for the price of a wedding ring and the name of Blunder to bestow upon the unborn child she carried.

I thought I saw tears gathered upon her cheek and, as I crawled away, my heart was broke.

I know not how that day passed, save for a pervading knowledge that I had been deserted by my sweet mother and was sick to every bone in my body.

Despite my sore head I had fixed upon Portsmouth as my destination and determined on entering the King's navy. I wore my work boots and coat and had snatched up a corn sack which I charged with a few turnips for my sustenance.

I was running away, trudging onward, unthinking of my sore feet. I was not driven by affection for a lost father, Miller, if ever he existed – for I now counted him a whim of my mother's fancy to bestow a semblance of legitimacy upon my birth when she had returned to Broadwell.

More likely I was inspired to run by a travelling Jack Tar who passed through the village a year since. Jolly he was, as befits a sailor, and his face mahogany or oaken from wind and weather. He was a fine figure, having been paid off with a grand share of prize money won by his ship. He took a fancy to me, with his colourful stories that stirred me greatly. Very well, I would be Andrew Miller, and turn my back on Broadwell and its doings.

Nor did I know the road to Portsmouth, except that it was eastward into sunrise or nightfall and I must avoid the highways. My late companions had discussed such points of strategy at our secret parliaments in the woods, whenever one of our number was in danger of being hired out to a remote farm. We had all heard stories of runaways being tracked by bloodhounds. They grew more lurid in the telling.

The shades of night were spreading when I bethought me to find shelter. The road was little more than a farm track and I had been afoot since daybreak with but a corn sack to keep the rain from my back. A black mood oppressed me to such extent that I cared little what fate befell me, but limped onward. To the left lay a scant plantation, scarce more than a hedgerow, and I scrabbled around for a hidey-hole among the tree roots to afford some protection from wind and rain.

Then a faint sound came again of a horse and carriage; its rumbling and clinking had dogged me all that day.

An owl hooted over my head and I started in terror – I who had lately been the bold poacher! It was quite dark now, and, had I renewed my flight, I had doubtless set up such to-do amongst the undergrowth as to carry the sound to my pursuers. I cowered beneath the sack, covering myself with evergreen sprigs, persuading my exhausted mind of my invisibility.

I failed however to find sleep until near dawn, The injuries and bruising I had suffered began to hurt in concert and, in misery, I imagined I was blinded in both my bruised eyes. The day-long flight had left my limbs a-throb and my left leg felt as stiff as an oaken post. Worst of all was the shaming vision of the attack on my mother and my failure to help her. As to its ending in her whispered submission over expelling me and binding me to labour on the starvation farms, my remedy was in flight.

Before the dawn light came I gave way to a restless sleep, not caring that the rain was flooding my nest, until a sudden rattling brought me upright and struggling from my pathetic cover. The only exit from my hiding place was blocked by a pair of shire horses, harnessed to a large waggon. I was accosted by the waggoner who peered from the other side of his great charges.

I stared sullenly, but decided he was no one I knew and unlikely to be a tracker in the pay of Richard Blunder.

He was burly in appearance, and though dressed in a

countryman's smock with leather gaiters at his legs, there was something about him that did not fit the cart drivers that I had seen. His face was weather-beaten but not in the way of a farmer, all pink and creamy. He was brown and his grizzled hair seemed to extend to his jaws in the fashion of some sailors I had seen. He wore his hair in an old-fashioned queue.

" 'Vast there, me hearty, a good day to 'ee," roars he, but, sighting my blood-caked appearance, he gives a low whistle and stares at me.

"You bin in the wars then?" he asks at last.

I peered at him through clammy eyelids, but made no reply. The newcomer examined me up and down, and turned to rummage under his canvas cover.

"A fanny-ful o' lobscouse would rouse your innards, boy – hot". In no time he had lit a small fire and heated a pot of bran and stew – and indeed I felt its warmth uplift me, whilst his chaffing banter betokened a friendly spirit. I offered half a turnip to add to the mash.

He was the utmost in joviality and made a person want to laugh with him, he was that full o' banter. It would not take long to take to his company, I thought, and I brightened at the prospect.

Little by little he sounded me out. I made no complaint, and all came out of a sudden when he shot a question at me.

"Running away, be you?"

"Aye, to Portsmouth, sir," I gushed forth, "To enter the King's fleet," and he was instantly on his guard.

"Nay, nay, cully. We ain't at war yet, and 'no war – no prize money', as they sez. What's more you be over-young for skulking round the yard with them man-o'-war's-men, and you'd be on boy's pay."

He seemed shocked, but, seeing no other future, I

persisted, so, saying he himself was bound for 'Pompey', as he called Portsmouth, he agreed I could ride with him.

And so we set forth, he finding me what he called a 'sleeping berth' beneath the canvas, of which he assured me I was much in need.

The route to Pompey, it seemed, was like the garden maze of Lord Seckberg's at Broadwell, a convoluted ride, which appeared to have no concern with haste. At any rate it took more days than I had bargained for, during what period I began to recover, and the bruises to fade from my body.

I rode on the driving box most of the time, swathed anonymously, at my new friend's insistence, in part of the canvas awning. "It'll shield you from whoever it is you'm clapping on all yer sail from." He had divined my plight, I saw, and I began to share my troubles as we jogged along.

We conversed amicably, and I told him my name and where I came from. He jolted me when he claimed to know about my village, but I had to believe him when he described it with accuracy.

His name was Bowlin, he told me – Ned to his mates. "And to them as is agin me," he laughed. He was like that – always chaffing and bantering, kindly disposed to all and counted a 'wag'.

At length Ned admitted that he had been a man-o'-war's-man himself.

"Now then, lad," he admonished me, "Why not take a shore billet until you knows something o' sailorin'? Aye, I knows a snug berth, an inn where all the admirals fetches up, and someone there as 'ould pay you fer the work, just the same as at the old Benbow's Head, eh?"

He took pains to assure me. "Goin' to sea is naught but 'ardships with naught to show at the end of it."

As we jogged slowly along, Ned regaled me with hair-raising yarns, which thrilled my soul rather than put me out, and he flinched not from proclaiming his deeds alongside famous admirals or captains. Then he would turn solemn and change his tack to underline the disease and discomforts of the life at sea.

"When you've seen all there is to larn on shore at Pompey, maybe I can git you on board a smart frigate as a volunteer, if you are still so damn fool wayward as to go to sea."

On our way we stopped at several hostelries, where Ned was received as a welcome guest, who called for many a cup of ale while conferring closely with his acquaintances, for all the world like a farmer at market bargaining to sell a pig.

He took good care of me with platters of game pie, hot from the landlady's kitchen, and saw I was bedded down o' nights.

In good time most of the stock he had been carrying had vanished from under his canvas and he steered the waggon into a remote farmyard to walk some distance away in close parley with the farmer. I was hustled indoors by a giggling farm girl who set before me an enormous dish of Swedes and potatoes, while the farm wife looked out of the window – tensely, as I thought.

With the farm girl seated by my side I made great inroads into the pie. She poured small beer from a jug whenever my mug was empty and I was well asleep before Ned returned with the farmer. Both looked wearied and bemired, but sat before another vast pie, eating and talking in soft tones. They had an air of conspirators, I thought, whenever I opened an eye.

There was much to-do about the farm kitchen until sunset had passed when Ned and I, accompanied by the farmer, set out on foot for a small inn. There, after a festive evening, with Ned doing the rounds, buttoning the inn's clients, we, all three, reeled back to the farm, where I could see no sign of Rose and Maisie, our horses, in the yard or stable, in spite of casting round about. At last I slept again before the open hearth, having not the wit or steady head to enquire further.

Next morning Ned was alert and upright, but disposed to be loud and hearty, and we trooped into the farmyard with the farmer, his wife and the girl, trying to look unconcerned at the new mixen heap which now topped the low outbuildings. I made to remark on its smell, when our two nags were led in by a Romany-looking pedlar. I could hardly believe my eyes, for they had suffered a change and in no-wise looked like our animals. They sparkled and gleamed with new grooming and, instead of black blazes to their faces and dark leg feathers, they now shone with white markings. They wore saddles and riding bits, and it came to me that they were now well disguised.

Once mounted on the shires, where I was completely at home, Ned shed his usual air of uproarious humour, and became surly and silent. I was filled with suspicions of something unlawful hanging over his head, and, of a sudden, over my head too, for it struck me that I was accomplice to him.

It was obvious to me now that the waggon was hidden under a vast heap of mixen and that the vanished stock which had disappeared in the rough farm country, needed explaining, for it might lead to hanging on the gallows.

But Ned refused to be drawn, and I was in a ferment of anxiety.

He had donned a long carrier's smock and gaiters, and on our ride into Portsmouth Town, where both farm people and maritime men thronged, he carried a riding crop to keep his mount out of the way of the waggons and carts that flooded both ways on the hill and led us down to the dockyard town.

CHAPTER 2

From the top of the hill I had my first view of the sea and the sails of craft moving in and out of the harbour. It made me hold my breath with the wonder of it. Beyond there lay a misty line of land, which Ned told me was the Isle of Wight.

As we got nearer Ned grew more guarded and suspicious, and I had leisure to see over the dockyard wall. There scores of men and boys engaged themselves in fixing long snakes of rope to the very tops of the towering masts.

I sensed that Ned's unease was become as great as mine. Indeed it seemed that it had grown larger these last few days, including the period when the horses were disguised and the cart hidden. For a public carrier he had attracted much more attention, even deference, than is given normally to men of that station. I had supposed that my new friend, having goods to sell, had possessed an air of greater authority than the ordinary run of drayman.

It was certain that when we encountered sailors that the petty officers amongst them had treated him as equal, when they talked – long and furiously – of ships in which they had served together. I must confess that I knew little of a petty officer's standing or duties. They had seemed mighty pleased to wager together at backgammon or other card games and it was 'hail fellow, well met'.

Even country gentlemen would take his hand with great jollity as though pleased to renew his acquaintance.

"Aye," Ned grunted. "There be a fever o' war spreading o'er the country, and a haste for to get the fleet to sea. They work double-tides, and rejoice to earn more pay. Soon the press may be abroad, but them dockyard mateys is protected against it. Seamen is fair game for the press gangs, an' when the war is done, they throw the poor 'tarpaulins' back on the streets – allus the same!"

We rode on in silence over the Ramparts, through crowds of townsfolk taking their evening promenades. Among them boy porters trundled handcarts, piled high with the baggage of sailors and soldiers, making their way to ships at the quaysides. I saw that their belongings might have to last many a long year before the owners saw Portsmouth again.

The throngs grew thicker and noisier around the shops and taverns, which were enjoying a thriving trade from marines and sailors, who had gained shore leave. They weaved through the crowds, bawling, "Halloo sweet'eart," or "Ahoy mate, what cheer?"

At last Ned guided us to the livery yard of a small inn where he led the shires to be stabled. Quickly he returned with a broad smile of relief on his face. He had shed the countryman's smock and gaiters for a seamanlike rig which consisted of a short jacket with a red kerchief at the throat and wide trousers. His plaited queue swung behind his broad shoulders as we walked on together.

"Lay on, Andrew, cully, let's get you to your berth."

We pushed through crowded streets, where lamps were being lit and the paving at the Theatre Royal was brilliant with more candelabra than I had ever seen. It was there that I stumbled to a halt, to feel my leg grasped above the ankle. Looking down I saw a legless beggar seated on the pavement, one hand held out in supplication.

"Spare a groat fer a poor tar as did serve his country at sea, young maister," he whined and the townsfolk hasted on past.

Ned swung round and the beggar released me.

"Oh, no offence, Ned Bowlin, I didn't know the young'un was wiv you, no offence!" And he quickly scrabbled backwards on some sort of trolley.

Feelings of pity and revulsion surged through me, to encounter a grown man toadying to a boy, but Ned only clapped my back and scowled, "Tcha, he weren't no tar struck down at sea, lad. He fell drunk under a four-horse waggon – just a bleedin' longshoreman 'e was! Ahoy lad, now here's real trouble."

A trio of highly painted young trulls, pushing through the crowd, thrust themselves in a provoking stance before us. "Wot cheer, Ned Bowlin?" cried one, and all broke forth into peals of giggling, moving away with good humour and bawdy taunts, when they saw he repulsed them.

"What about the young'un then? We'll larn him free o' charge." They affected to collapse in laughter again when they saw my blushes.

Ned glared at me, but I kept my thoughts to myself, This city was a veritable eye opener to me and I wondered that so many knew Ned by name.

We came to a corner, where a sign proclaimed 'High Street', turning past a large house with a red-coated marine sentry standing guard.

"Residence of the Port Admiral", said Ned.

At last we came to the sign of the George Inn, a house of three storeys, whose large portals were encumbered by the London coach, 'The Regulator'. The street was a-ringing with the last strains of the post boy's horn, and a crowd, disgorged by the coach, was about to have its thirst slaked by serving girls with large trays of ale mugs.

Ned smacked his lips in anticipation, and I could see the landlord bowing obsequiously to the more affluent of the passengers. Several parties of seamen, some with midshipmen at their head, filed amongst the new arrivals, seizing the baggage of uniformed sea officers to whisk it away to their ships.

Ned led me to the side and through a quieter entrance. He pointed down the street with a warning.

"Old Portsmouth lies that way, lad. Take care if you have to go down there. You'll run across a rough crew, an' no error, 'specially at the sign o' the 'Blue Posts', where the young gennulmen o' the fleet go for shore grog and vittles afore they slips for sea. They'm a mite boisterous."

To me the whole population of Portsmouth seemed a mite boisterous, and on the point of departure.

The George's taproom was more subdued and frequented by a humbler clientele, intent on ale in the fog of clay pipe smoke.

A young serving girl in a coarse apron, by the name of Rosie, squealed in surprise when Ned summoned her. She brought strong drink for him and small beer for me, chaffing Ned for being absent so long, while she eyed me up and down.

Suddenly it was as if a whole gale had blown through the room, and Ned got to his feet. "Doll Dooley," he bellowed and the whole company looked up as one man. A robust, handsome woman threaded her way through the crowds of wherrymen and porters. Her ample gown flowed behind her, beneath a vast mob cap, from which gingery ringlets peered out.

In a loud voice she demanded where the 'divil' had he been, deserting his one true love, and she clamped him to her stout figure to the cheers of her customers, while demanding aloud to know if he had any notion to make an honest woman of her.

Of a sudden she swung round on a surprisingly slim ankle and peered at me.

"And who, pray, is this young sprig?"

Drawing her to one side Ned whispered in her ear. His harangue lasted some time for I was but one of Ned's concerns and there was much else to say. At last Mistress Dooley turned on me and bussed me in her soft bosom.

"Ye're as welcome as the marnin' dew, darlin' boy, Oi bin lookin' fer the loikes of you for these two or t'ree month – so Oi have."

She led me away to the back stairs, throwing out orders for this and that, and, in no time I was assigned a berth with real blankets under the stairs. Thus I was installed as pot boy, and to run errands for the George Inn, for four shillings the month, my keep and any tips from the guests I should serve.

CHAPTER 3

I was to learn much of Pompey in the next weeks and months. As the seasons passed, its noise and bustle grew ever louder as the rumours of war multiplied.

Of this I heard much talk in the taproom of the George. The dockyard men, coming in to sup jugs of ale, were old hands at judging how the affairs of France would affect their work on our ships in reserve for it was but three score miles from the Needles Channel to France.

The French had rebelled against King Lewis to demand equality for all – from peasant to king. In large numbers, his noble families were flying to England for safety. The Queen of France, Marie-Antoinette, was a daughter of the Austrian emperor, who was drawn into war when the mobs of France imprisoned her with the royal family. For once Britain seemed set to remain aloof from Europe's travails.

We heard that the new French troops, the revolutionaries, had swept aside the finest Austrian armies and now threatened Holland, and our Baltic trade. "Where will we get our masts and pitch now?" the shipwrights and riggers protested.

All this talk filled my head with a conflict of emotions. It made Broadwell seem more remote. There, we were wont to hear little or naught of the doings of foreign kings. We cared only for the harvest as the seasons marched by in stolid sequence of lambing, sowing and reaping. Lord, how I yearned for it.

Of a sudden I pined again for the rural excitement of poaching with my fellows, of outwitting the keepers, and catching the eye of the Queen of the May at our annual fair.

It was a different emotion that filled my breast at the

sight of a first rate ship entering harbour, anchor at the cat-head and her reduced canvas ready to catch any light breeze. Below, her three gun-decks bristled with iron muzzles, and aloft there were topmen who filled my soul with admiration while the measured chant of the leadsman was a new wonder to me.

Like Ned, I now confess to being drawn either way, betwixt the slow seasons that ruled the countryside and the immediacy of action required of the ship's crewmen.

As a year passed, and then another, the George claimed my day relentlessly from dawn to well after dusk. Its demands were not unlike those of the Benbow save in urgency and length of the day's work. Mistress Dooley, known to everyone as 'Doll', was the housekeeper and took charge of life below stairs. It was said she ran a taut ship.

I cannot say that she favoured me with the best of errands, but, since the inn boasted a service to ships in the harbour, I was set, with Ned for my schooling, to man a clumsy dinghy, to handle the oars, cope with tide and wind, and carry my fares on board their ships. When I became handy at this task, I found that I could earn high tips, dependant on the fare's state of sobriety.

I became familiar of the quays and landing stages on the Gosport side as well as of the ship berths at the Dolphins and creeks, Whale Island and the rest. It gave me a confident air, and I was resolved to join a ship as soon as Ned should give the word.

Then I should be free of Richard Blunder.

It was now the year '93, after a French general, flushed with victory at Jemappes, demanded that all kings should be executed and England, in particular, invaded and ravaged. He demanded that 'trees of liberty' be set up in every English field. His outburst caused the more uproar here since he referred to that villainous machine, the guillotine – a blade used to cut off the French king's head, and all Europe shivered at the venom of the ragged-arsed armies of France.

Now Mr Pitt declared war, and King George, proclaiming that he was proud to be an Englishman, determined to be at the head of his troops to meet the foe, removing himself to Weymouth on the South Coast.

For centuries, the townsfolk of Portsmouth had been accustomed to providing the warships for the country's first line of defence, the Navy. But the brutal slaughter which had broken out in France was now on everyone's mind.

I was kept busier than ever as my rounds of Portsmouth grew in number, and new men flocked to a town girding for war. Ned had warned me of ways to keep an eye open for the press gang, but it was of no avail to Ned himself as we learned.

"You'm been growing fast, and there ain't a man in the ships' press gangs as wouldn't take you for a servant or a landsman's billet onboard of any old scow that floats. Doll says she'll look arter you, but once you bin taken, it's a task for God almighty to set you free".

Doll's plan was to sew brass plates on the inn servants' sleeves, showing them to be protected from the press gang, thinking one engraved for the George might serve that purpose. After all, the inn was almost part of the Navy.

Ned sniffed at her optimism.

The time-honoured equanimity of preparing our ships for sea at the outbreak of war, was rudely broken that year on a mist-laden day in the Solent, which be the channel separating the Isle of Wight from the mainland.

Often had I viewed the array of ships moored in a great bight across the water and growing in number almost daily.

Their anchors held them against the winds and the tidal stream which scoured them, east to west and back, twice a day. Most lacked vital stores and all wanted for extra hands and were encumbered about with tenders and rafts.

Late that day a number of merchantmen appeared through the mist from St Helen's Bay in the east. They came from a long-expected convoy and nothing was remarked, save their unwonted spread of canvas in a foggy area of banks and shoals.

Yet soon it was seen that they were under chase!

Behind them (or astarn, as we say) there appeared a cloud of strange sail, fast luggers, firing their guns to harry the convoy, which, one after another, handed its sails and wore back into the fog, like sheep before the sheep dogs. The great men-of-war at the Spithead were helpless, having no means to bring their artillery to bear on the intruders. The very impudence of the luggers' men in closing the British fleet showed how well aware they were of its impotence.

Portsmouth burst into a state of belated terror, fearing the worst in its streets. "French corsairs," they cried in panic. They need not have worried, for the raiders cared only to escape with their prizes, the merchantmen, undamaged and were now well on the way to St Malo or other ports on the French coast.

However red-coated British militiamen wheeled out their field pieces, artillerymen sighted their cannon on patches of mist, while small cutters gave chase in futile haste through the Needles channel in the west. All too late – the stable door shut dismally.

Then followed a period of varying fortune, mostly of mishap, in which Ned and I suffered various reverses or triumphs. Aided by the efforts of journalists and reporters, or retired generals in the council chamber, the French corsairs had made the folk of Portsmouth, indeed of the whole of the south coast of England, keenly aware of their positions. A stringent guard was rowed nightly round the partly completed warships at the Spithead, and ship owners, with vessels awaiting convoy in the Kentish Downs, set up such a furore in the House of Commons as to speed the reinforcement of the fleet.

The down-Channel convoys began again to sail past St Malo and the Seine, on course for the East or West Indies or through the Straits to the Levant, always under heavy escort.

It surprised me to realise that near three years had passed since I became a pot boy and inn servant in England's first naval port, where the headlong scramble to war was affecting all the citizens of Portsmouth. Only fortune had kept me from the clutches of the press gang. Ned was likewise in danger and about to fly into the cover of a ship of war for fear his skulduggery, already discovered, should suffer further leakage that would leave him swinging at the end of a rope.

The Impressment Act was passed in record time. Officially it applied only to sea-faring men, though these were in great demand by the merchant fleet as well as the king's ships and many a merchant jack's pay was already raised. I decided it was high time that one Andrew Miller set sail.

Many French naval officers had resigned or fled into exile in England, while their navy lost its highly trained maritime gunnery corps, thrown ashore in the name of 'égalité'. The naval base at Toulon had mutinied, enabling Lord Samuel Hood to invade the port, with all its ships.

"Should not all this be to our advantage?" I asked Ned. He nodded, but broke fresh news that had not yet reached the Portsmouth journals. Ned possessed a nose for contrary tidings, thought I.

"Not all, cully. The Frenchies ha' taken the Dutch fleet, – just galloped across the ice, and the Dutch joined them meek as yer like in their frozen harbours. And down south the French army drove Sam Hood's ships out of Toulon wi' artillery atop the hills. And they're threatening to plant trees o' liberty over here, or 'guillotines', as they calls them."

The horror of King Lewis' execution surfaced later when his Queen met the same bloody fate.

Doll gave me a new task about this time. It was to paste up the press handbills, summoning:

"All stout-hearted British tars to repair to the George Inn, there to meet Lieutenant Goodheart, and drink a toast with him to his Majesty, King George, with damnation to his foes and all murderous revolutionaries who would make slaves of us all, and bring ruin to our wives and daughters. Volunteer now, my hearties, and snap up prizes at the drop of a hat – Britons Awake! God save the King!"

Known seamen of Portsmouth were sought high and low in the houses and taverns backing off the main streets, and many with commitments on shore were seized, despite protests.

Captains of frigates generally had no trouble in filling their complements, in particular those that had come by enemy or neutral ships with contraband cargo of value. In the early stages of the Great War, there were merchantmen at sea with no knowledge that a state of war existed. These ships were stripped ruthlessly of deep-sea hands, leaving only sufficient to get themselves into harbour. This, occurring within sight of land at the ending of long voyages, was decried as brutal.

The press gangs were now become so loathsome that riots developed, with women and children a-stoning the sailors, in fights to save their loved ones. Apart from sentiment, a wife might lose her husband's maintenance and have to turn to others for support. There were magistrates who would attempt to arrest the pressing officer with writs of habeas corpus.

I learned to walk the streets with caution.

"It don't signify for an old hand like me," said Ned with bravado, "a true man-o'-war's man' don't have no wife 'anging round 'is neck, but 'uman nature being wot it is, the mess deck gets cleared for women to come on board in 'arbour. And a scurvy crew they is – bum-boat gals and street walkers, my lad – up to all sorts o' tricks."

He spat and blew smoke down his nose. "Young lads, like you, should never see such a circus."

I smiled secretly to hear such hypocrisy

That very night, Ned was to see the end of his free and easy life under Doll's wing, free food and drink, and free concealment from the press gang. Now his past sins were about to catch him up.

He had never confided in me further than that he had been employed as a draymen, a carrier of Naval stores for the Yard. It gave him protection from the press, though the gangs might easily have ignored it once they got wind of his previous naval rate as bosun's mate in a first-rate.

The multitude of stores he had collected were sold illegally and his tracks covered by a plot, in which the normal driver was subjected to a false attack and found with convincing injuries. I was reluctant to believe it of my friend and mentor, but what I had heard, bit by bit, seemed to tally with his doings on our winding road to Pompey. I wondered whether to consult Doll for advice.

The housekeeper called me to her before I could act. It was but to carry the bags of a naval lieutenant up to his room, in and out of the way corner of the top floor. We had better rooms, better located on other floors and I wondered if he had somehow found disfavour with Doll for some reason.

His name was Usher, I learned, and his foppish dress and haughty manner, seemed to answer my question. I received no reward for my labours for him either.

This lieutenant did not frequent the usual circles of boisterous, hard-drinking young officers, though like them he was assumed to be waiting for his ship. He disappeared of evenings into the hurly-burly of Pompey life.

By day I was sent several errands by Usher, mostly to a tailor's shop in an unfashionable quarter, and on another occasion I was instructed to take a note to 'Hellfire Betsy's.' I had never heard of such a person, and said so, but Usher, who was in his cups, raved at me so offensive, that I fled below to take Doll's advice.

She was deep in a wrangle over the prices for strong drink, and waved me away with a literal answer. "It is Number 92, so it is, and tell that Betsy she owes for a dozen o' best champagne."

I went, puzzled.

No. 92 High Street cowered behind a shroud of ivy. All to be seen was a pretty bow window and a half-hid door, which I tapped with due circumspection. It was flung open to emit a be-cloaked, bent figure who brushed me aside, disappearing into the darkness.

Behind, an immensely bloated lady, of some years and clad in a voluminous gown, hair all pinned about with faded feathers and baubles, peered at me with suspicion.

Hastily I thrust Usher's note into her hands. "Wait boy," she commanded, then shrieked over her shoulder what sounded like "Forward, Jenny." I glimpsed the low-beamed hallway was ill-lit by guttering dips that smoked and spread a deep miasma of cloying sweetness as thick as a Channel fog.

'Hellfire' shrieked again for this Jenny.

There ensued a clatter of high heels (as I subsequently discovered), and in a scarcely concealed screen of complaint, a dark-haired young lady appeared. The newcomer was dressed in gaudy finery of the latest mode. Nestling amongst her dark curls, there were glimpses of large gold hoops and I trembled with pangs of rueful admiration for the pouting mischief of her dark face. She reeked of a sweet savour.

"Fancy gent," purred the fat lady, "Wanting you partickler, dearie. At the George. Boy will take you."

The girl smiled at me and winked hugely.

"Ah, the dashing lieutenant, is ut? Come then, boyo, off we go?" She grabbed my arm as if I were her beau, and it tingled with a sensation of elation, as we walked all the way up the street.

"And don't forget my cut!" bawled the fat lady after us.

How long Jenny remained in Usher's room, I cannot tell, but on later occasions she would jest that I was her particular sweetheart, flirting with sweet kisses and laughing at my discomfiture. However much I sorrowed at her profession, at nights I dreamed such dreams in which she was ever just out of reach, and mourned desperately.

Working as a page, potboy and messenger at the George was a sure path to learn the ways of the world.

On one of my errands to the seedy tailor shop I took a pair of Usher's topboots to be refurbished in the deep band of gold lace and a gold tassel at the top.

The tailor was an ancient Jew, known as 'Shimey', and as I had been respectful to him on my previous visits, he took to asking concerning Usher, probing, as I first thought, for the prospect of his bills being met, but it was much more than that. I showed him the boots and he sniffed, "not the boots of a sea officer, hey?" I agreed, I had not seen their like.

"This goy Usher, mein boy," he said at last, his eyes twinkling and his wispy grey beard floating as he spoke. "He gives you a good tip for all your errands, yes?"

"No sir, he tips nothing," I replied indignantly.

"Oi yoi, sonny, too bad, too bad."

He rubbed his hands in an agitated fashion, and I was sure he had not been paid for all his alterations. He bent his old head towards me and paused nervously.

"He uses mein shop for a message drop – you say nothing, you hear me? Sometimes t'ree, four men meet together with Usher, émigrés, you onderstand – Froggies, you say – spikking der French, so."

I knew not what all this signified, but the old man thrust a cutting from the Portsmouth Recorder, concerning a man, name of Fellowes, killed under the hooves of his horse. He was an old sailor, a disabled lieutenant turned farmer.

"Thees man vas here also, but alone. He vas, how you say, frightened. Usher and his friends had lodged at his farm, and zey found him listen to zair talk, in French. Sadly he onderstood them too vell, oy vey."

Shimey pointed to a pair of pantaloons, hanging from a beam, of which one leg was complete, but the other ended below the knee and was gathered into a wooden peg. "Mister Fellowes' leg was shot away at von of your sea battles – vat use have he for horse, at midnight? His housekeeper swear he have no horse in stables!"

"He vas killed, I tink, – the hoof marks over his face were stamped by hand-job, eh? Vas easy."

Collecting Usher's precious boots, I started hastily to seek Ned's advice, but turned back to ask if I might take the news journal cutting for a friend of mine. Shimey nodded, trembling, and I took his arm.

"Mister Shimey," I stuttered, "You should shut up shop and go to a friend for safety. Please Mister Shimey." I was convinced he would comply.

Back at the George I learned that Ned was out for the night on some mysterious errand. I lay, half asleep in my bunk considering my fate. It seemed certain that Usher was in some dangerous intrigue. Was he a French émigré like the rest of the group at the tailor's shop appeared to be in Shimey's eyes?

Heavy steps above my head and low voices snapped me back into wakefulness from the first words.

"Aye, that's him, name of Bowlin," came the first voice, in low-pitched tones.

"Then this is your place. You'll know 'im by 'is moleskin vest and 'is Jack-me-hearty talk – spends most of his time here with Doll, the head wench, but I see her a-serving in the tap "

"Enough, I know the cut of his jib. You take station here, while I cast around the place. If he comes in, stop him civil-like, but no set-to. This place is full o' cocked hats and gold lace up aloft."

"Aye, aye," growled the first voice, and both sets of feet stumped to the foot of the stairs.

I pulled on stockings and breeches and carefully slipped out of the cuddy into the shadow of the staircase. A burly man in a red woollen hat stood at the side doorway. 'Voice, the first' guessed I, but the second was nowhere in sight. Fleeting glimpses of Doll appeared, as she swung a tray full of beer mugs over the heads of her customers. I told her quietly what I had heard.

"Steady, my love. Ned ain't here," she whispered in my ear. "Go to the 'Golden Cross' now. Sure he'll be there in the back taproom, if I'm not mistook. Now, don't be rushin'. Where are yer two men?"

"One in a red cap is at the side door, the other went in I think."

"Well, that don't sound like the press gang. Now go on, go on – tell Ned, without raising a hue. Say, I'll be casting me eye around. The whole Ring is in danger." The Ring, a highly lucrative and secret consortium of robbers, had preyed on the dockyard stores for years.

Ned Bowlin, just where Doll had prophesied, was in converse with two villainous-looking fishermen, rather than the serving wench that Doll suspected.

"Avast there young maister, you'll have me on me beam ends," laughed he at my headlong approach "What's afoot?"

I whispered in his ear, adding that I thought they looked to waylay him.

"Do they, by George? Come, lad. Let's clap our eyes on these swabs, afore they sights us."

We set out for the inn.

When we arrived, Ned, peering through a side window of the George Inn gripped my arm for a moment before stepping out.

"Sink me if it ain't Red Danny! Wot cheer, shipmate?"

Danny wasted no time on the niceties. "You'm wanted by Mr Chissel, Ned Bowlin. Just bide here whiles I fetch 'im!" He returned before Ned could collect himself, and I saw he was put about. Behind Red Danny, a tall man in a long, caped riding cloak appeared out of the shadows.

I was waved away but managed to remain within earshot. Mr Chissel, a man of great presence and few words, stared at Ned.

"Jig's up, Bowlin," his voice harsh, just above a whisper, which was the more threatening. "It was your private play with cart and horses that spiked our game."

Ned nodded acceptance of this without a word. But his face was white and serious.

"If the law takes you, they will uncover the whole Ring." Chissel stared unblinking. "The High Sheriff's agents have cited you – fancy disguises won't save you from the gibbet now. The Ring has gone into recess for a year or so, and has chosen you for foreign parts, from under the agents' noses. See to it." As he started to walk away he added softly – "do not fail the oath."

"I'll not cross your hawse, Mr Chissel," came Ned's bold voice as the tall man vanished into the darkness outside. From then onwards events sped past both of us with ever increasing speed.

In the minute's silence that followed, I tried to gain Ned's attention to the tailor's obvious terror of that afternoon, and waved the news clipping under his nose. Eventually he listened to Shimey's fears, and, his face clearing, he smote one fist into the other.

"Aye, that Usher! He's to be the admiral's flag-jack - joins the *Queen Charlotte* tomorrow, I fancy. What's this about his boots?"

I showed him the decorated footwear, and a smile crept over his face. "Old Shimey, eh? He knows more about the flag officers and captains than any of us. I cannot see Black Dick taking to them objecks on 'is quarter deck – them tassels is only wore by horse hussars, I'll wager – only good for fouling the rigging in a wet gale. And, now I think on it, this Usher is a replacement. The man appointed was waylaid by footpads on 'is way here – shot 'im dead and 'e wasn't found for weeks, hidden in a gutter."

I supposed I should have not have been surprised at this display of his knowledge of naval affairs, but all I asked was "who is 'Black Dick?'"

"God luv us, lad. He's the new commander-in-chief – arrived today to hoist 'is flag in the *Queen Charlotte*, Lord Howe by name, but 'e's Black Dick to the fleet, dark of face and silent as the grave – he'll call me to mind. I was 'is cox'n once, and must get a berth in the flagship tomorrow – safe from them ferrets from the High Sheriff."

Ned hadn't overlooked my account of Shimey's fears. "Right and proper job, what you said to the old feller, Andrew. I'll get somebody to listen to it. That peg-leg devil, Fellowes, was flag jack to an admiral onc't, and he knew the signal book back to front – but there's a new one now, which Black Dick 'isself wrote down – there's a coincidence, ain't it? One thing certain is Fellowes couldn't mount a 'orse, even before 'is leg was shot away. Shimey was dead to rights there.

"Now I must stow my sea chest for tomorrow, and get to the Guild'all fust thing. I'll give you a call for we may need a runner tomorrow, eh?"

He aimed to get paid a bounty before his disappearance into the navy.

He clapped me on the back and I turned wearily to my bunk for the second time. My mind was a-turmoil and I got no sleep.

CHAPTER 4

Ned departed without arousing me, and I heard that he got early to the Guildhall through the back lanes, to be entered as an able seaman in the flagship *Queen Charlotte* which was crying out for hands. Doll, who had walked him down to the ship at the quayside, told me that he had sworn to wed her – but she had heard that story many times.

"Damn fool, the man," she stormed, "to call at the Guildhall and claim a volunteer's bounty – five guineas, and now he's shipped as AB, when he should be a petty officer, the bosun's mate." She dabbed her eye and I saw she truly had tender feelings for him, as she bustled off muttering under her breath.

The next news I heard was from Ned himself, calling in the George's tap. He seemed to have a free run as a veteran hand in charge of shore working parties and I ran to see him with news that Usher was nowhere to be seen in the inn.

Ned merely nodded. "I come ashore on dooty," he said. "And who does I see on the gangway but Sir Josiah Probyn – big man in the dockyards 'e is – talking with the flag captain. I tips me hat to both on 'em, an' Sir Jos says to call me to him later, as he is acquainted with me from the old *Leandros*, to which the flag captain agrees like it was perfickly normal."

He went on and on about Sir Josiah's fame as a 'nat'ralist', and his studying of plants and wild animals, the world over. "Mark you, he'll be known for that, long arter this little spat with Monsoor Frog is fergot."

I was to learn later that Probyn was head of the Admiralty Intelligence, but his joy, which he seldom confessed, was to take part in missions in the field – to share the dangers of his agents. He held the post of Director of Dockyards, as a cover for providing his easy access in naval circles.

Ned drank up his ale, kissed Doll with gusto and he was off, nodding to me as if something was afoot.

I caught a brief glimpse of his bustling figure in the George some days later, but only learned that he had been rated bosun's mate in the *Queen Charlotte*, from which Doll deduced that he could stroll ashore from the pontoons more often, being the bosun's right hand man.

It did not transpire as Doll wished however, for both Ned and I were to vanish from Portsmouth in a circumstance of violence which, after all these years, I still regard as being the start of our adventures.

It started as a trivial, even pleasant, occasion on the road to Southsea, a new village attached to Pompey's side. I went there on an errand for a guest at the George, and on my return across the common, the noise of crowds and music came to my ears. In short, it was a new regiment of foot that marched towards me, heading for the camp at Eastney.

The evening sun lit the scene of massed red-coats, headed by the trilling music of fifers and the 'thump, thump' of their drums. I had been pondering the fate of 'Shimey', as I must call him, and cursing that I did not ascertain his future whereabouts.

I was oppressed also by fears of the mysterious Lieutenant Usher. He was not on board the *Queen Charlotte* yet, according to Ned.

As the soldiers drew nearer I pushed my way into the cheering crowd, to gawp as file after file marched by, exchanging banter with the young girls who waved them a welcome. At the rear came a procession of light carriages, open to the evening air, some with be-feathered senior officers glaring with distaste at the mob, and, at the very rear, some curricles bearing young ladies. Mounted officers of the younger set surrounded these last vehicles, flaunting their horsemanship, flirting and tattling almost beneath the parasols of the ladies. Occasionally they doffed their caps to an imagined acquaintance in the crowd and, through this conceit, I found myself staring into the eyes of Richard Blunder.

At the sight of his bared head of straw-coloured hair, cut short in the latest mode, there rose in me fresh waves of fear and loathing. In a flash, however, he had replaced his cocked hat and the encounter was closed, as he renewed his addresses to one of the ladies in the vehicle. Suddenly I saw that this lady, the object of his attention, was my mother. I reeled away in confusion.

On my return to the George, I sought out Doll and laid the afternoon's chance brush before her. Fortunately the matter of the Blunders' of Broadwell had been gone over by Ned and Doll a number of times of late and we all knew of the threats of banishment posed by the farm hiring fairs.

Doll was not dismissive of my story, but inclined to think my fears could be a fancy.

"Sure, an' 'tis them spliced and wed now, d'ye not see? Didya see a wedding ring, boy? Yer ma will be lady o' the manor by now."

She paused to dramatise the event.

I had never put any faith in the notion of my mother's marriage into the Blunder family. Though beautiful and of genteel nature, she had been a poor woman all her life, while rich men were known only as philanderers and seducers, according to the boys of the poachers' parliament back home. Of certainty, young ladies had to obtain family consent to marrying and succeeding to a fortune.

When I had seen her earlier, I had supposed she was a lady's maid travelling with her mistress.

Doll cast her eyes heaven-wards in disbelief, but admitted it was a possibility. On saying I was unsure if Blunder had seen me, she sighed deeply. "Divil the boy," she spat, crossing herself fervently.

I told her firmly that I must go into the Navy at once, and, at this, the old baggage cozened me along with a pretence of agreement, after my sea-chest should have been mustered – and she'd see what Ned should have to say.

Secretly I determined to brook no further delay – the press might seize me at any corner. But first I was in want of a volunteer's bounty to fit me out with a seaman's kit. Besides I saw that I had grown too old for a youngster's employment.

At the Guildhall I was seen by a clerke, who treated the bounty money as though it was within his own personal gift.

"I fear I cannot find a place in a frigate for you. Such ships require hands of great ability and knowledge, lad. You shall have to go into the *Queen Charlotte*, a first rate she is, indeed my Lord Howe's flagship. They will knock ye into shape there."

I said naught.

With that he scribbled at such length in the pages of a great ledger that I, seething with anxiety, could have supposed that he was apprised of my every imperfection, which he wrote down for the eye of some great admiral.

His face rolled with sweat under an old wig that had fallen askew so that he resembled a pug dog, about to bite.

He looked up and found I still awaited him.

"Yes!," he barked, and I summoned all my nerve to request my bounty.

"Bounty! Oh, is that what you come before me for – a bounty, eh? Not for the glory of serving His Majesty in the finest ship of all the world. Wait there."

Another hour passed but I had grown stubborn. There had been none other awaiting the clerke's attention, and I was on my own.

"Come sir, I wish to volunteer; is there no end to your labours to man the King's fleet?" I demanded loudly.

The clerke turned a purple hue, choking to find his word.

"Do you expect the sum of one whole guinea to be placed in the hand of any Tom or Dick who presents himself before me?" he spluttered.

At this the door opened and stilled his growing torrent of words. "And what, pray, is your business, sir...?"

It was Ned, arrayed at last as befitted a petty officer. He glared at the clerke, plainly displeased and boomed. "Avast, cully, this lad has been three hours of the forenoon watch here. He is required on board for instant de-fumifying a rat-ridden mess deck. My Lord Howe is seriously concerned that the servants of 'is good friend, the Mayor, cannot find the urgency to conduct the business that his ships require. And you sir, pray acquaint me with your name!" I grinned behind my hand.

In only a minute I emerged from the little office, the proud owner of a slip worth two whole pounds to be accredited to my pay in HM Ship *Queen Charlotte*.

"A longshoreman's bounty," pronounced Ned, drily.

A further matter was to be attended at the George, which was set in motion by a string of serving lads and girls. It was to mark my entering a ship of the line as a seaman, this being attributed to my waterfront service as a skiff man, well-known in Portsmouth Harbour.

There was the prospect of advancement to able seaman, once the bosun was satisfied that I was capable aloft, and the quartermaster that I could steer.

"An AB must hand, reef and steer, lad, before he can be rated," warned Ned.

Although I had learned the knots and splices from him, I would have been more confident had I set a foot on board a ship at least once.

A runner came to the George to warn Ned that hands were required early next morning to prepare the flagship for shifting to the Spithead, that Mr Shaw, the senior warrant officer and ship's master, had returned on board from his home in Gosport, and that bosun was expected hourly. It was a fine gesture of his mess mates – or perhaps a warning against his too frequent absences. At any rate Ned became as sober as a judge on the instant.

He looked at me. "Outside, lad, with that sea-chest o' yourn, and call young Spiker. He's handy in the dinghy and we need 'im to bring the boat back to the Camber."

Spiker also proved handy, helping to carry my sea chest to the small dock, called the Camber, where we kept the boat. He did the boots at the George, but, forever envious of my boatman duties, he had a broad smile at my leaving and Ned was to give him a tip for his help.

That worthy was seated in the stern sheets, while we two lads settled on the single thwart to row. The waters sparkled with reflected lights from ship and town, and we fumbled the oars to their rowlocks in the darkening fairway, when with a loud crash Ned was flung to the bottom boards with a great oath in his mouth.

The dark shapes of two men had dropped from the dock walls and the boat near capsized as they sprawled on top of the floundering Ned. Spiker and I were bearing off, beneath the dripping net of mooring warps from other boats, when I saw that both men had large pistols.

"Pull after that boat ahead, you boys!" snapped one of the newcomers in a voice of authority.

"What in hell…" Ned struggled upright but, sensing the situation, cut off his outburst. The cloaked leader flourished his pistol, growling, "Officers of the law! Look lively – there are French spies in that boat ahead."

Ned seized an oar and added his weight to that of Spiker and me to send the skiff skimming over the still waters, following the dimly seen splashes of our quarry. A flash illuminated all our faces as the pistols cracked sharply. The boat ahead changed direction instantly.

Soon both boats had passed the bows of the *Queen Charlotte*, and headed towards the Gosport side of the harbour and into the creek, where the new naval hospital dominated the dark fields of Haslar.

Panting at my oar, I noticed the rushes whipping past as we ran into shallow water. Spiker was entranced with the excitement of the chase and squeaked in my ear, "Pull man, pull!"

The boat ahead had slewed on a mud bank, and the law officers stood to take aim. The flat spitting of guns drew forth a scream and a great splash from the chase, where the fugitives were trying to scramble through the shallows. Ned and the two officers leapt into the water and splashed to the stranded boat, while Spiker and I pulled our lightened skiff through reedy channels.

Two of the men heaved a dripping figure back into his boat, which, after being man-handled through the weeds, was taken in tow by the George's skiff.

The leader of the law officers rejoined us, there being no sign of the man he had chased ashore. "I have asked the hospital guards for a search, but have no great expectations of it," he told us.

Now it was time to get ourselves to the *Queen Charlotte*'s gangway, and we feared our arrival at this late hour would run us into trouble, but Ned begged a word with the law officer who understood our fears.

He willingly agreed to inform the flagship of his requisition of our dinghy and our services in hot pursuit of villains, and bethought himself to thank us for the same.

"Well done my lads. I 'ull see you do not lose by it. I am acquainted with your flag captain." In boat's bottom I spied a glint of metal and found a soaking tassel which I pocketed, saying naught. I would show it to Ned, and explain my fears, as soon as might be.

Back at Portsmouth we landed our lifeless capture on the hard for the cloaked officer to search his pockets more thoroughly. "French!" was all he said, and we pulled the boat to the *Queen Charlotte*'s gangway.

This is how I entered the King's ship, with many a delay which had to be explained, but also it came to notice that I was possessed of at least longshoreman experience, and on account of it was entered in the rate of 'seaman.'

Before Mr Shaw, the ship's master, I was questioned about my doings across the harbour in a private boat. I answered truthfully but made no mention of a signal lieutenant of the admiral's staff. Perhaps the questions were put merely to judge if they tallied with Ned's story.

PART 2 – BLACK DICK IN THE CHANNEL

CHAPTER 5

The *Queen Charlotte* came to her mooring at the Spithead. She was at once surrounded by tenders of all kinds and the work of stowing their contents below was back-breaking, the day long.

As a seaman in the ship's books, I was to be paid at nineteen shillings the lunar month, the victuals found or an allowance instead, being messed on the lower gun deck. There I was thrown in with the most colourful mixture of rogues and innocents ever to be imagined. This mess became my home.

Despite my seaman rate, they recognised me as a 'cully', or an awkward and ignorant hand. I had picked up much from Ned, but my place on board was as a new born babe's. However, when a draft of landsmen came from the receiving ship, I saw how advantaged I was and supervised some at the tying up of boats and lighters.

All the messes was wedged between the guns. The sacred mess table, a home to about a dozen or so hands, was triced up to the deckhead before the guns went to action.

At moorings in a tidal strait we were not troubled so much with the eternal problem of wives, but bum boats flocked round the ship and much was smuggled through the gun ports, especially in the way of strong liquors. Beside, various traders were allowed on board, to buy and to sell, for there was carving of scrimshaw and model ships by the crew to trade and much more.

Life in the mess decks brought a family feeling along with it. Before the fleet quitted Portsmouth, which was anticipated by all to be soon, we had regular deliveries of postal packets. It was in the 'dogs' one evening that AB Davey came asking for a quiet word with me. He was a lively youngster, sharp of wit and a well-loved wag who was friendly to all – a cox'n in the ship's boats.

His lips worked but no word came as, dumbly, he handed the sealed packet to me. It was obvious that he wished me to read of some private catastrophe and without further ado, I commenced in a low voice.

He was to learn from me – alas – that his girl, a house maid in London's Pimlico had lost her employ once her state of being with child had become signally apparent.

"We was to be wed next time I am paid off," Davey growled. "Sweethearts we bin since we was childer. An' I swear I ain't bin near 'er this twelvemonth nor more."

I went on reading. This madam had found free lodging with a Mister Volski and his troupe of dancing girls, and she was earning good money conducting country bumkins round the sights of Vauxhall gardens, where some of the girls made small fortunes at the game of dalliance.

At this last revelation Davey's face hardened and he snatched the letter from me.

"Enough, mate, I'll think on it."

He departed grimly without a glance astern, leaving me to marvel at his lack of reading. Of course he came to me as a friend, to avoid patronising the mess deck 'scribes', who charged a fee for writing replies, and were thought to be a source of banter and wounding wit. But he required me to make no reply.

Now all gave way to the daily exercise of the great guns – without live charges – being as we were close to the town of Ryde and to friendly shipping. I was fortunate to be spared the gunners' way of life by virtue of being in the bosun's part of ship. At least I thought as much, until I learnt that my station was exposed to enemy fire in battle, almost equally with that of the officers on the quarterdeck. My duty was to tend the foremast sails, the headsails, on deck and aloft and to clear the anchor.

Mention must be made of the pervading smell on the mess deck, namely of 'bilge water', the perfume of which is like to remain in my nostrils to the day I die. In return our victuals entitled us to more meat in four days than I had at home in a month o' Sundays.

I found the seamen were at odds with the 'idlers', who had no night watches to keep, while we were divided into the starboard or larboard watch. As you may expect, I saw little of Ned, except when both watches were mustered just after dawn each day, and divining that he must not appear to have a favourite, I kept clear. It was in order, however, to take up with 'Welsh Yanto', who was rated master's mate, for we often worked together.

Yanto was a year or two older than me, and I first admired his easy prowess aloft. He had some little authority too, being equal to a midshipman, as everyone admitted. We came into contact first on the fore topmast shrouds where my foot was jammed and not to be extricated, as I judged, without pain.

From the deck I received orders to 'lay below at once.' My struggles to do so only worsened the pain, but I refrained from a shouting match, especially as the officer of the watch was showing interest.

It was then that Yanto came springing aloft to release me, and help me below.

He touched his hat to the officer, offering an explanation about slack futtock shrouds that went a good way to absolve me from any blame and I was sent forward, hobbling, to the sick bay, but it was naught.

Days later it was Yanto who raised the alarm as the day became light for the morning watchmen, discovering a bundle of canvas suspended from the topgallant yard, 'hanging Judas', which is to say 'swinging.'

It was found to contain the body of Davey, hanged without a word of explanation forthcoming from all the enquiries made thereafter. I informed only Ned of his distress and no more was heard of our dear messmate, save his interment ashore, which the captain decided should be attended by the men of his mess. Many there were who grieved at his loss.

Of course, life went on as normal. At noon when hands were piped to dinner we took turns in our messes to draw the beer which replaced the rotten water. It was a delicate task, for undue dispute was made of any spillage. It was worse when rum was spilled. Each day the 'cook of the mess' took the meat ration to the galley and strove to make it the more tasteful with spices bought mostly from bumboats. Fish, caught over the side might be taken instead of pusser's meat. The ships' cook would put the whole confection in the coppers.

After such meals the messes erupted in the boisterous wrangling that settled many a dispute and spawned more, while the 'spreading of buzzes', often occasioned wagering on the most hazardous of chances.

The gentle reader must accept that the lower deck man was generally unaware of intelligence which might wreak havock on his life and limb tomorrow or the day after. Often your common Jack was not privy to the bombast of the news journal, and never to the dispatches that arrived constantly for his captain's eyes, but the 'buzz' often repaired this deficiency for the lower deck man.

Most commonly a pearl of scandal was spread by the eavesdropper, in particular the dumb servant who served at the officers' table but kept his ears abroad, or the savant who could tell the signs. They have been known to spread news of a destination, unknown even to the officers and sometimes to achieve a degree of accuracy.

One buzz was passed round the sceptical lower decks of ships at the Spithead. It was boasted that a signalling device from hilltop to hilltop could cause a ship to be dispatched to sea from Portsmouth within a quarter hour of its being decided in the Admiralty. No one believed such nonsense and the betting was mighty thin for once.

A break in storing ship, repairs aloft, and the everlasting gun drill, came now.

"You may see Black Dick sooner than you thinks," Ned assured us, "allus stand ready and don't go breathless when you're called for three cheers. 'E's a good hand – seen action at sea since the year '40 I believe. I reckons he'll be hoisting a new flag soon – as Admiral o' the Red."

He did not say it was already on board – and Ned, 'the savant', had seen it.

After a morning of cleaning and painting ship we were dismissed below after dinner to don our best rig for the fleet commander, Richard, the Earl Howe.

Unlike the sea officers and midshipmen, there was no uniform for seamen then, although the fleet's pursers bought clothing, or 'slops', which was generally alike. Many buyers of these slops made alterations to suit their fancy – by ribbons added to sleeves, or hats made waterproof with tarpaulin – presenting not too motley a crew.

The admiral's barge was sighted emerging from the narrows of Portsmouth harbour. We could hear the merry ring of church bells and the firing of salutes all round the eastern Solent. Our new lord and master sat in the stern sheets below a red ensign, which denoted the senior squadron of the Navy.

Gold lace glittered on his uniform, though it cut a strange dash, for he wore blue breeches instead of the usual white. His bargemen pulled a steady stroke across the tide. On board the side party blew silver calls in unison, rising to a high note as the barge drew alongside, and another ascending note until he stepped into the starboard entry port.

It was the famed 'Piping of the Side'.

Black Dick raised his cocked hat as the marines in their scarlet coats, presented arms. The admiral looked about the ship briefly with an experienced seaman's eye, moving back to see his flag broke at the main truck.

In the silence that followed he read out his commission and was presented to the sea officers and the master. The brief ceremony ended as this spare, elderly man became the main defender of a Great Britain facing invasion.

At the quarter-deck rail, he raised his hat again and gave the order 'to splice the main brace', to re-doubled cheers, for it signalled an additional issue of rum.

Discreetly in the old man's wake came Lord Howe's aide and flag lieutenant, his eyes darting from side to side under a plain cocked hat. With a start I saw it was Usher, and my mind churned over the ways to unmask the suspected murderer and spy.

In expectation of an early action against the French, our newest hands were confused about their roles and Ned took, every opportunity to school them. Drills under the captains of individual guns were a great help of course, but his talks of manoeuvres in wind and weather were often too complex for many to follow.

"What else is the new signal book for?" Ned asked the assembled messes. "Mark me, lads, the line o' battle as 'ad its day, no matter what the Fighting Instructions say."

As the fleet's captains returned from convoy they were summoned to discuss tactics outlined in the new book.

It was not only within the Navy that such disputes raged. There were letters in the news sheets, leaflets in scurrilous language and public discussions throughout the land. Even clergymen held forth on naval tactics and, now that France threatened invasion, the uproar grew apace.

"The line?" you may inquire, "and pray what line is it that arouses such pother?"

For answer I must crave the astute reader's indulgence to digress. The 'line of battle' was a formation of ships, designed some centuries before to preserve a fleet from attack by an overwhelming number of the enemy. Ships of the line took position so close to the next ahead, that the enemy could only attack at the sides where the main batteries could blast them.

Should one fleet overtake the other's line, its guns might be clustered against a smaller number of the enemy rear and overwhelm it, before its admiral could turn his ships to bring them succour.

Nor could a commander devise an alternate strategy, for the line was demanded by Admiralty order, to break which could bring awful punishment.

If both fleets formed rigidly in line, there was danger of a drawn battle ensuing, with great damage to both fleets. To prevail in battle the guns below and the sail aloft had to be handled more speedily than the enemy's, hence our drill, drill, drill. Contrarily, both sides aimed to capture enemy ships with little damage to masts and hulls, in order to earn a greater sum when later sold as prize.

New hands sat silent as the tales were told of past battles under this admiral or that captain, and of the prize money earned. Good cheer abounded whilst the beer flowed, for there was always a goodly ration. Many had to be helped to their hammocks long before 'pipe down.'

There was a good leavening of faces of all colours and creeds in the messes, and, indeed, many languages. Some came from farway lands and sat – silent men – save for a few bold souls with a smattering of the English tongue, who understood the history of the 'foreign devils' and that their battles were not topics in which to join. The men of Orkney were fine seamen too, but preferred their own silent company, unless it came to a fight, which they considerately held on shore when they had some pay. There were also Irishmen who, we all believed, held their own Parliaments in dark corners.

Black Dick himself was respected as an ancient hero who smiled only when going into battle, but he was kindly disposed to common sailors and trusted by them.

CHAPTER 6

A means of keeping sailors informed of family news was furnished by the ship's postman, who collected mail on shore for the ship, for officers and for ratings. There was considerable traffic in letter-writing from London, where even the lowest servant girls were wont to read cheap books from the halfpenny libraries that abounded there.

In due course 'Postie' declared that a package came for one Andrew Miller, lately of Broadwell. It was from an attorney who wrote that my grandfather had died, and the farm was left to me. In a corner away from the mess, I shed a tear for the old fellow with whom I had worked, learning much about the agriculture of the new age.

A second note from the attorney declared that he was ready to serve me, in the matter of the land at Westwell, which grandfather had inherited on the death of his brother, my great uncle, and his kin which would also come to me once probate was granted.

I saw that such an event should have brought great joy to the recipients and their kin, but to a common sailor it must present an intolerable burden also, due to his confinement at sea.

Strangely, the attorney made no mention of the future of the Benbow's Head but there was another letter, saying grandmother had been removed to be under kindly care, her health being of the poorest. My mother, it added, had made arrangements for the inn to continue its trade.

The writer was Mistress Golightly, the young lady who had taught us to read and write at Broadwell, and my heart lifted at the thought of her tender and caring nature. Most of my young comrades at her evening school had fallen under her spell too, and treated her with the greatest respect, a rare enough attitude in that herd of rogues. If it was out of a helpless adoration for her young beauty, who could be surprised? I must confess that an equal, hopeless, fascination had stricken my own breast.

She now lived with Lady Seckberg, she said, and would I please to write to her there with messages for my grandmother. She intimated that Lord Seckberg was aware of my bequests, and would correspond with our captain if I wished it.

Of her husband, the curate, she made no mention, and I supposed she had employ as companion to Lady Seckberg, for Golightly was not inclined to provide much sustenance. He was known rather for his miserliness.

According to Ned, Lord Seckberg had served in the Navy as commodore, and was likely acquainted with our flag captain. "Watch him," said Ned, "He's a taut hand."

Strangely, I tasted a feeling of being under the thumb of strangers who deprived me of my freedom, but I trusted Mistress Golightly, who ended her missive with best wishes and prayed for my well-being on the sea. Thus began my habit of letter writing.

At this further expression of kindness I determined to write to my grandmother at once, as a means of prolonging a connection with home. The news put upon me the most immediate problem of the farm's husbandry. The beasts would need feeding, and the neighbours would attend to that for some time, I trusted, but I thought the cultivation too much to burden them with, neither could I expect my mother to intervene. I needed an agent and Lord Seckberg was the natural man to turn to. I remembered that he had given help to my grandfather with seed and tools.

Life below decks was often rent by complaints against

officers or petty officers. Coming on board one day, I ran into such an instance. The corporal of the gangway whispered a warning – "Watch out, cully – officer of the watch!" There seemed no occasion for the warning, and a splendid apparition in snowy breeches and silk stockings passed by without a glance.

The corporal relaxed. "Snotty bastard, the Honourable Rupert, ain't he – our new fifth, a real green'un, by God."

This brief encounter served to put me in my place, for the officers, I divined, were a class apart, to whom we paid servile obeisance, despite the fact that we were shipmates in one hull together.

It brought to mind my grandfather telling me to draw aside for a gentleman's coach which bore down upon us in a narrow lane, spraying us with mud. In pushing me up the steep bank my grandfather was knocked down by the coach's wheel and he cursed the departing carriage, at which it pulled up, and a grinning postillion beat my grandfather horribly with a whip, while the old man sobbed 'keep your place, boy'. All the heart went out of grandad at this humiliation ... and now he was gone.

I cannot tell whether a similar chasm exists between officers and men on board – certainly the hands refer to officers as 'pigs', though we are all shipmates together.

"Depends on yer captain," says Ned.

Post came thick and fast and my next missive was a tiny note smelling of violets which caused much ribaldry when Postie flourished it in the mess with great ostentation.

Once more I retired and discovered it was a weepy letter from Rosie at the George. It was the greatest of surprises, for she was swearing undying love, and I recalled guiltily that we had kissed at my farewell. Hastily I stowed it in my pocket, and strolled to my mess with an air of complete nonchalance.

I was greeted with a howl of laughter, and the bawdiest of jibes, till my face burned scarlet. For days I was sniffed and sighed over, as if I was a garden of violets myself.

On the day following I was busied in the vilest-smelling compartment in the ship, the bosun's locker. There the barrels of slush were stowed, with paints and Stockholm tar, to be readied for 'slushing down', which is for keeping the weather out of the standing rigging. Slush is bought of the ship's cook, being the used fat after the meat is boiled in the galley coppers. We hated the stink of it.

The bosun's mate summoned me. He carried a packet in his hand, and, telling me to scrub myself, said he had another letter come on board. "This 'un is from Doll. I been expecting great things from the dear wench."

Surely enough the letter proved to be from Doll, whose round Irish hand he had recognised. She related how she had visited the army camp at Eastney, on the pretext of selling wine to the officers' mess. She found that my ma was indeed wed to Captain Blunder, who had purchased a regular commission. She was now styled Mistress Blunder of course, and had quarters in the village nearby with a nursemaid who tended her small son, named William. Her husband spent most of his days at infantry practice.

My own existence was not mentioned. I could understand her life had changed, and such neglect was expected.

That was not all. On her return from Eastney, Doll had traced the housekeeper of the late Mr Fellowes, formerly partner in the small farm. They had taken as lodgers, three or four men with Scotch names and, being herself a Frenchwoman, she was struck on overhearing their guests discoursing privately in French. She could not say if aught particular was discussed, but would think on it.

So I have a new brother, may God bless him, I thought. Happy for my mother, although so distant from my world. Later, we heard from Fellowe's housekeeper, the French mam'selle Meg. She had found a stout wooden stake hidden in a ditch. One end was weighted and a bloodstained horse shoe lashed to it. She had immediately travelled to the coroner's residence in Portsmouth to show the weapon to his assistant. He showed much interest and told her that the corpse displayed a knife wound to the kidneys.

"We shall bring in a verdict of murder," he assured her.

Doll's motherly salutations, to which were added Rosie's prayers for my safe return, ended with an entreaty that I look after Ned, which turned the 'buffer' red in the face, and musing aloud that we needed to find old Shimey.

Ned was ashore next day on a special mission, they said, for the flag captain, name of Hamlet. I saw he wore his best rig with a watch coat, and his rough exterior had changed to something approaching a smart turn-out.

When he returned in the first dog watch, he took me on one side with the news that Sir Josiah Probyn was now apprised of all the information we had from Shimey and Meg, but thought it was no proof against Usher.

Admiralty records had Usher reporting his last ship to be the *Lark*, a sloop, taken by the French after stranding on the rocks of Brittany. The French Ministry of Marine had not reported the names of her crew in custody.

It was always a slow process, often withheld for political motives. Then an exhausted officer adrift in a small boat, giving the name of Usher, had been readily accepted by his British rescuers and by Admiralty, who confirmed his status as a survivor.

Ned, however, was satisfied that grounds for suspicion had been sown. The following day he asked me what had connected Usher in my mind with the boat chase across the harbour.

"It was dark as the ace of spades that night," he remarked.

I related my story of picking up a gold tassel from the bottom boards of the spies' boat that night off the Hard. It had been on my mind, but I was afeared my story might travel around the ship afore we were ready to act.

Ned stared. "You did right, lad. Tell me these plans o' yourn."

"About that boot tassel," I said, "Usher's servant must find out if its fellow is missing, but the lad is right afraid of officers, and might let the cat out of the bag."

At this Ned himself sought out the servant with all the bustle of a frigate making sail, saying he would pay a tip. At this the boy confirmed one tassel was missing.

When the Portsmouth news sheets appeared on the streets, we were astounded to find that Lord Howe was attacked for remaining at moorings in the Spithead. A well-known scribbler came in a hired boat to speak to him. He had to climb a Jacob's Ladder and along the boat boom, amongst the flour bags and the sailing hoys with vegetables – victualling was in full swing. On board he was received with scant welcome and kept waiting while strings of sailors barged by under heavy loads.

Eventually the captain of the fleet, Sir Roger Curtis, appeared. "Ha Mister hrrumph, you have an appointment, I believe. No! Then you cannot see Lord Howe, sir! Perhaps I can enlighten you – I have but a few seconds. You are concerned, I collect, with the presence of our ships in the Solent, and believe that they should be elsewhere, is that not so?"

"An idle fleet does no good in prosecuting the war, sir…" commenced the scribbler.

"Aha, you are not suggesting that these fellows are idle, I presume – see how they toil and sweat. There are nine hundred souls to feed here and as many in other ships of the line; it may be twelve month before we return to the Solent. What, pray, do you suggest we should be about?"

"Why sir, to protect our merchants at sea -"

"At two this very morning His Majesty's ships *Defence* and *Glory* sailed with 128 of merchantmen in convoy… does that answer to your requirements, sir? The Trade will be protected past French ports from Ushant to Biscay, safe from the Frenchman's navy, because it is locked in port. For tomorrow's convoy there are other sail of the line, who stand ready as escort and so on."

He turned away, and giving orders for a jolly boat to carry the newsman back to Pompey when one could be spared, he wished him a very good day and vanished.

It was known that the Earl was chiefly concerned to discover French plans for invasion, and to meet them at sea. Despite that, his ships were disappearing with convoys. His captain of the fleet, meanwhile, explained future tactics to the captains as they came and went. All this time fishing vessels were chartered into the fleet to speed ships in their refitting.

More responsible tasks were put upon me once the slushing down was finished. There was a shortage of ABs still and I was told off for messenger to the bosun's mate of the watch on the gangway.

Frequently this was a tedious duty, but sometimes relieved by helping secure or move the lighters and hoys alongside. Working for the Navy was a welcome task also for most of the west country fishing skippers. It doubled their pay, you may reason, for they still fished the night long and I observed that some took advantage of the ease with which they could filch from naval stores.

One Devon fisherman contrived to come by a new suit of sails, which stood out from afar, as it formed a distinctive pattern of white at the peak amidst the normal red-brown below. She was called *Paynton Rose*.

Early in the morning watch, surprised to find Lieutenant Usher on deck aft, I watched him closely. He carried a leather pouch. I had a strange feeling that something was about to happen, when *Paynton Rose* came closer with maddening slowness.

Usher took no notice of her until she had almost disappeared under our counter. There was a sudden movement and slapping noise as her mainsail swung across. Usher was moving aft, and the noise of the cutter going about stilled as she glided quickly away on a new tack. I swung round in time to see Usher disappearing into the coach, where he had a berth.

He was no longer carrying his leather pouch. When I turned back there was no sign of a pouch on the deck of *Paynton Rose* either.

So that's the game, thought I.

But the other pressing matters on my mind had troubled me all the night, half-longing to be rid of these underhand doings and back at my native Broadwell. At the muster of both watches I stood fast. Fortunately my watch was to be dismissed to lay below, where I could catch Ned's eye and I asked how one could speak to the flag captain.

How it happened I do not know, but by the middle of the forenoon watch, the servant of the captain's secretary came on to the lower gun deck, accosting me with a brazen air. He was but three feet away when he lifted his voice and bawled, "You! – Seaman Miller – you'm to report to the sentry; captain wants you – sharp, matey!"

Every head on the main gundeck turned and stared and I cursed silently, for this impudent boy had let the cat out of the bag. Everyone would want to know of it, now.

Fortunately, I was seized by the captain of our mess' gun before I reached the ladder, and he hissed for me to fetch a cap and a clean scarf and collar, while he himself ordered the queue I had grown. He pushed me to the ladder and grunted what I took to be a wish of good luck.

My rig must have passed muster, for the captain's secretary murmured approval and ushered me past the sentry into the cabin, making sure that the captain's pantry was empty of eavesdroppers. I was relieved mightily.

Captain Hamlet commanded the flagship, a much younger man than I expected and, as I stood before him, he seemed to sum me up in a trice.

"This is a happy meeting, Miller, and we must shake on it." He smiled broadly extending a hand for me to take,

"Damn it, Sidney," he turned to the secretary, "It ain't every day we have a double landowner in the cabin, hey? Why I believe we may drink on it; young Miller is about to miss his midday wet."

I collected that he had news from Broadwell, and felt that he put me at my ease.

"Now, what service can Commodore Seckberg perform for you? He is a friend of mine who cares deeply about the new agriculture, for I hear there are riots in London over the price of bread – it is the drought, I'm afeared,"

"The ploughing is my first concern, sir. I thought Joe Young of Broadwell might take it on. He is a friend who has worked on the land – and well-known to Lord Seckberg, who might wish to keep an eye on him…"

The captain smiled broad and I stopped for fear I marked Joe for a poacher...

"I'm sure he will do, sir."

"Just so, Miller. Allow me to write to Lord Seckberg, and good fortune go with you. Now, young man, I hear you have been of great help to Sir Josiah Probyn – who will be sailing with us. He tells me that you have proved to have a keen eye. I want your word that nothing of this business will appear in the ship 's scuttlebutt!"

I nodded fervently and he said that he had in mind to rate me a master's mate, after a short apprenticeship, if I was willing and showed promise. I thanked him awkwardly in my surprise, and he warned me again of the need for a tight lip, but that I might confide in Bowlin.

CHAPTER 7

When the time came for departure from the anchorage, it was early in the morning watch. The ships' companies of all ships, watch keepers and idlers alike, were already turned to, for the Spithead was about to be laid bare, save for a few ships still to be repaired.

The Flag was going to sea.

As I passed through the gundeck I perceived our great anchor had not been got out of the sea-bed's grip, and the going was hard for the capstan gang. The lanterns set the shadows of half naked men, growing taller, then, shorter as they dance round the ship's walls, bent low to the capstan bars, until the whole machine turned its endless hemp messenger about the deck.

The anchor cable was seized to the moving messenger by boys bearing stout yarns called 'nippers.'

At my station with the bosun's party forward, all was tensely silent. Ned, perching above the ship's stem, acted as the bosun's eyes to report when the anchor is aweigh.

Only Shiner White, the leadsman, kept up the monotonous chant of his soundings for the master, who conned the ship alongside of the captain. To windward on the quarterdeck there was a glimpse of Black Dick.

At the expected call "thick and dry for weighing," the boys clapped on more closely to meet the greater strain that came when the anchor broke from the ground. Then the distant call came of "anchor's aweigh, sir," and the strain of six hours' hard work was lifted.

The *Queen Charlotte* moved in the water now and forecastle men, waisters and after-guard formed lines on deck to let go or haul the falls of running rigging, ropes which moved the sails of their appointed mast. All was under the orders and curses of their petty officers, for no one was at rest.

I looked aloft and saw the white sails, curved to the wind, and the topmen of the bosun's party aloft on the fore topmast, and thrilled with nerves and the anticipation of it. Though my duty presently was on the foredeck, I had to take my turn, if I was to be rated master's mate.

At last the flagship was free of the land.

Ships of the van, flying the white ensign of her admiral, were to lead the way through the Nab Channel, and, once we had sea room, we would expect to form in line of battle.

Occupied as we were, I felt relief at the absence of questioning about my visit to the captain, and discovered that as the sea got up, the wind being against the tide, a vast discomfort had assailed many of us new men, and all interest in food and other topics had diminished. Our only consolation was to pass into fitful sleep in our hammocks. The old hands seemed immune, and I was sustained by a hope that the sea sickness would soon pass.

Alas, from there our wretchedness was increased as the watches were called and we reeled on deck again in weather unfit for a dog. Sail had been shortened by the previous watch so there was no immediate danger of our working sail aloft, until I was told off for lookout

I went gingerly to the foot of the weather shrouds, where Ned came close to me and passed the small telescope used by lookouts aloft. "Don't ee look down, me 'andsome," says he, "use the lubber's hole, and take the lee side o' the top – speak clear and loud to the officer of the watch if you sees anything. We ain't in formation now. Good luck!" With a clap on my back, he was gone.

How I survived that watch I scarce know. Fervently I

had hoped for a 'quiet trick' but the low mist prevailing made the task nerve-wracking, for I saw nothing in the wild movement of the mast, which bore the top way over the ship's side. A longing for my hammock assailed me.

In the mess our misery was made worse by the leaking of the lower gun ports as they rolled under the waves, and the welter of loose mess traps that slid one way or the other o'er the deck. Ned appeared at every muster, giving sage advice and laughing, "There's an old saying –

'When wind comes afore the rain
 Soon you'll set your royals again.'

How we longed for that day.

Within a couple of days we were tacking from the French coast to the English against a head wind from the sou-west, but it had calmed down to light airs with a hot sun overhead, all of which meant slow progress. The fleet which had been much scattered, was in formation once more, and we commenced sail drills and firing broadsides at targets, until the Channel resounded from side to side.

Aloft, I was gaining confidence as a top-man, and had begun taking landsmen aloft to show them the ropes

The Flag and all the captains meanwhile had much practice in the use of the admiral's signal book, when it needed to detach ships of the line to take convoys round Ushant and further south. All in all we had gained much from the disruption of the gale.

My thoughts, however, turned to the farms and I longed for a letter from Joe, or, more ardently, from Mistress Golightly at Broadwell, and my face fell at the thought of her. Thus the fate of all departing sailors.

Still intact, the fleet passed Start Point well to the southward, and those who had wagered on Torbay were dashed. "So, Plymouth it is!" gloated the backers of that port, as they set about extracting their dues.

They were to be disappointed, however, for Lord Howe had determined to see for himself in what strength the French navy could get to sea. Their main base was in Brest, which was in an inlet called the Gullet, a short way eastward of the rock-strewn passage of Ushant. In the frigate *Speedwell*, he ventured within sight of the harbour, with all the experienced eyes aloft assessing the state of the French ships, especially to see if their yards were crossed and dressed for sea.

The French were used to the sight of British ships setting foot across their doorsteps, we reckoned, for Brest had long suffered our blockade, but Black Dick followed that by turning and sending probes into all their Channel ports, even some hidden behind rock-bound, twisting channels, where our small, armed, tenders were used, at great risk from guns ashore. The fleet withdrew, not without a fair assessment of the French preparations.

Meanwhile, the messes seethed with those who had paid their bets demanding their money back – because our course was not set for Plymouth. Those who had fancied the chance of Torbay being the fleet's destination were jubilant now, and crowed over their opponents, as gamblers will, but there's many a slip.

A heavy fog enveloped the fleet which came to open order at once and took in much sail but began to lose way. The wind was in fickle gusts, mostly from the south, and there was much boat traffic, including one bearing a Mister Bowen, master of the fleet, who came on board of us from another ship, to be met at the gangway by the Earl Howe.

While boats were lowered to tow astern and bearing-off

spars readied in case of collision, Black Dick conferred on the quarter deck with Mr Bowen and Sir Roger. The three men were old friends and Black Dick looked to the fleet master for a lead.

"This will be a long job, I think, Mr Bowen," Lord Howe remarked. "Tide is slack and no glimpse of the coast – I believe we are closing it."

Mr Bowen nodded. "Start Point is close ahead to larboard, admiral. I recommend no alteration of course in that direction at present – not enough sea-room. All ships to bear away on the Flag's quarter in open order, for we shall need to pass further orders, no doubt."

"What else, sir," barked Black Dick.

"Send the *Black Joke* inshore sir, to take a bearing and report back. She is just astern, and can be directed by speaking trumpet." The *Black Joke* was the ex-fishing vessel which was now the tender to the flagship.

"Sir Roger," nodded the admiral and the chief of staff departed with a nod in return.

"Can we reach the *Speedwell*, sir?"

"By boat," replied the terse commander-in-chief. He trusted the burly master entirely, and called for Captain Hamlet to man a boat.

I had been standing as quarter deck lookout but in the mist had seen only shadows that faded in the swirling vapour. I was now ordered into the boat as lookout. "Admiral's compliments to *Speedwell*, he's to drop astern to speak the Flag. Pipe the gig away."

Thus began a period of high activity which I shall never forget, rapid, but orderly, for every man knew the fleet was in danger of stranding – and all Black Dick's flags could not save England from a disastrous consequence.

Black Joke disappeared into the mist as directed, while the frigate *Speedwell* was ordered to take station five cables ahead of the flagship, just in sight, illuminated by a makeshift display of red lanterns in her after rigging. All the ships nearest in the formation were to send boats to their next astern and so on down the line – open order was to be kept.

The gig, commanded by a midshipman, was returning to the *Queen Charlotte* as the *Speedwell* wore round to her station and narrowly avoided running us down.

Black Joke closed and reported the bearing and distance of the Start. She was ordered ahead of *Speedwell*, but closer inshore, displaying a similar cluster of red warning lamps. Our way was abominable slow.

The tide turned to a more favourable set but the mist remained till near midday, when we saw Start Point clear to larboard and orders to steer for Torbay were hoisted.

I was sent for by the ship's master and Sir Josiah Probyn in the wardroom. Mr Bowen, master of the fleet, was there, but it concerned *Black Joke* only.

"Ah, lad," he turned a great jovial face to me. "This was my doing. I hailed *Black Joke* with instructions for her to go inshore, and now need to make sure I was not dreaming in that mist. The captain of her seemed to throw his voice from aft to the fo'c'stle head. Did you notice a canvas about round his leg?"

I said,"I thought it was a medical dressing. It was the mate who hailed us forward." I asked where the cutter had gone.

Mr Bowen raised his hand as if to prevent a to-do, and remarked that Sir Josiah had asked she be returned to Portsmouth – "no more questions, if you please, Miller, and be assured that Bowlin knows of it."

I left them, puzzled at Sir Josiah's interest. Mr Bowen's face was a study – plainly he wondered if boys had charge of the Channel fleet.

By mid-afternoon the first ships reached Torbay, a pretty anchorage encircled by low hills with the harbour of Torquay reserved for the senior officers' vessels, and awash with ships boats, all claiming to have urgent need to get ashore. On the mess decks we heard that many villas had been taken by the wives of ships' captains.

It soon became apparent to the common hands that we might just as well have remained at Spithead – "so near yet so far," I mused, but the buzz was abroad that Black Dick himself was to sanction a modicum of leave to one part of a watch each day if ships could spare them.

Once again we were greeted by peals of bells from all the churches surrounding this peaceful haven. I wondered if the appearance of a new 'town' of wooden-walls, of perhaps twelve thousand men, set down in their midst, would alarm the local populace, and Black Dick would doubtless have to go the rounds of mayors and lord lieutenants in the next days to set their minds at rest.

There was no doubt about the absence of Lady Howe, for she had duties of her own as the senior lady-in-waiting to Queen Charlotte. It was rumoured that Black Dick might forbid even senior captains from sleeping ashore. Torbay had been chosen as the best berth for falling upon the French if they ventured out from Brest, which usually happened after storms had driven away the hardiest ships of the close British blockade, the 'Inshore Squadron.'

I was now taking turn as coxswain of the jolly boat, and found a familiar figure stepping into the stern sheets on a sunny afternoon. It was Yanto in his best turn-out as a master's mate. His appearance caused the crew to nudge and whisper, until it was time to depart, when I gave the orders to make for Brixham, a fishing village on the other side of the bay. Postie sat in the foresheets with his bag, watching all, and mischief in his face.

The oarsmen, being familiar with both Yanto and me, had taken liberties with boat's discipline, until I had to tell them to hold their tongues. "Officer in the boat," I cried. "Now give way with a will or I'll see that you tilt your caps to the gangway officer on return."

Yanto looked away red of face. The crew knew that he was to meet his bride at the Blue Anchor in Brixham, and, of a sudden I felt absurdly envious of his mission.

In the evening the jolly boat was sent into Brixham again, to pick up Postie and the mails, and we saw Yanto turn away from his young wife.

Whispers and smirks flared again in the boat as I walked along the mole toward the mate. "Boat alongside sir", I called, touching my hat. He showed great surprise.

Back at the boat I turned on the crew. "Pipe down, damn you. It is Mistress Davies, and don't forget it." I snapped in annoyed tones. "Oars" The crew took up their oars meekly enough, avoiding even to steal glances at Yanto's weeping bride, and I wondered at my savage mood.

Yanto was first to board the flagship, in accordance with naval usage, but, as Postie stepped over the thwarts, he looked mockingly at me. "And how's your sparking with the good curate's wife a-goin', Miller?"

I was stopped, speechless, and wondering at my passion and even fear at what pain he could inflict and I could say naught, should letters from Mrs. Golightly dry up.

Next forenoon, Yanto edged along the fore royal yard to where I was hauling the sail's head to the earrings. He stopped short about a fathom from me, and said with simplicity, "Thanks, mate."

We laboured away at the sails, descending to the lower yards as each task was finished, when the mate stopped me and pointed out a frigate hauling into sight round Berry Head. Carrying her sail until the last minute, she rounded to and her anchor splashed at her foot, a signal for her sail to be handed in one almighty rush. Her captain descended into his gig and, to the wail of pipes, was pulled toward the flagship. It was all smartly done. It took longer for her yards to be squared though.

Amidst the fuss of manning the side below us, the squeal of pipes and the appearance of our flag captain on deck to greet *Nymphe*'s captain, Yanto grasped my arm.

"Time for us to lay below, matey," he whispered, and we sailed down the backstays to the deck.

PART 3 – BATTLE OFF PRAWLE POINT

CHAPTER 8

There comes a time when all is headlong rush and hurry; and this occurs more frequently in the King's ships than any other station of life that I have seen.

It is sufficient to say that the lives of a dozen 'Charlottes' were set to be transformed. In only a trice, we were racing down-Channel – that is to the West – on board the frigate *Nymphe*.

Our mission was simple. *Nymphe*'s new captain, Edward Pellew, was woefully short of men to man his command, even to sail in search of a crew, and his purpose was to recruit from the unemployed miners of his native county of Cornwall. Though it was a captain's task to man his ship, he had obtained Lord Howe's consent to borrow men from the fleet, and all was set in train in one afternoon at Torbay.

It seemed that Yanto and another mate from the *Royal Standard* were to be in charge of the borrowed men, and Ned Bowlin was our petty officer. In addition to helping the *Nymphe*'s sail to the West country, our task would be to train the Cornish miners in handling sail – they were reckoned to be already at home with gunpowder.

Yanto had been primed beforehand, I suspected, probably by the flagship's master, Mr Pryde, but he said naught.

Truth to tell, most, if not all, the hands went with a good will, for Captain Pellew's reputation in the matter of prize-taking had gone before him.

We were given little time to shake down in our new ship. She carried thirty four guns on one gun deck, and most of us were astonished to find how much closer we sat in the sea. Her speed, her motion through the water and her thoroughbred appearance alike, raised our hopes of taking prizes, before we should be returned to our ships.

Pellew's luck was with us from the beginning, for we made a record passage to Falmouth harbour, with sail and gun drill all the way, until we were ensconced amidst green hills, and let go our anchor under the shelter of Pendennis Castle.

Needless to say, our commander was on his way in the gig to clear his activities with the local big-wigs, and within a few days we were receiving boatloads of mining and fishing men, who were to man the *Nymphe*'s guns. Most of the mines had been laying off men with experience of explosives, and the fishermen were on hard times too, but it was the name of a Falmouth man, Pellew, that drew most of them to a King's ship.

Before long near 100 men had been signed on – a surplus, which Captain Pellew was anxious to take to sea, to select the best men. We cleared the Lizard Point and set course for the area south of the Scilly Islands, where the great Atlantic rollers met the shallower waters at the Chops of the Channel. The new men of Falmouth were at the guns or working aloft at all hours of the day.

Ned was mightily amused by the surplus of hands. "Black Dick done a good deal with Pellew." He guffawed. "Blessed if *Nymphe* ain't over her frigate's complement now – I'll wager the line o' sail will get any hands over the two hunderd and sixty mark."

When *Nymphe* had looked into many of the ports on the French north coast, bombarding where warships were within range, she turned her bow for Torbay to discharge the borrowed men. At dawn she was nearing Start Point when the foretopmast lookout made the fateful chant, that changed all our lives yet again.

"Deck sir! sail right ahead, sir, rounding Prawle Point, Frigate sir, thirty six – French, sir."

A sharp command of the officer of the watch caused the ship to resound to the rat-a-tat of the drum, beating to quarters, and preceded the thunder of feet on the decks and curt orders to gun captains and their crews. Pellew's training, brief though it was, would soon be put to the test. My heart beat in time with the drum.

"Deck sir! Frigate is *Cleopatre*. She mounts extra chasers fore and aft – wearing the new colours of France, sir," intoned the lookout.

To the master, Pellew said, "As soon as we have her larboard side in sight, I mean to run down on her, larboard to larboard, and pin her against the tide race round Prawle. Ready the larboard broadside, Mr Pellew."

"When our broadside is fired, master, I mean to wear to starboard, so that, if she turns for France, we shall at the least be to the south'ard, though we lose the windward station. Ah, Mr Brandish."

The lieutenant of marines stiffened and crashed to a salute, his grotesque, heavy sabre clanging on the deck.

"I wish to clear *Cleopatre*'s quarterdeck and then stand by to board. Mr Pellew will see to it that the disengaged gun crews follow you, and, after them, the topmen, as soon as they have secured the enemy's yards."

"Very good, sah," Brandish would have saluted and stamped again but the captain had moved off, "Master, bosun, when the ship is wore round, stand by to clew up the fore and main, so that we can turn in a smaller compass, then re-sheet on the instant to come hard on the wind again."

"Aye, aye sir."

Nymphe's maintop was already filling with the sharpshooters of the marines, and bristled with their rifles behind the barrier of tightly lashed hammocks. Youngsters were bringing shot to the guns and strewing the decks with wetted sand. The tools of the gunners' trade were pulled down from overhead, and the captain of each gun was testing his flint or firing locks.

Water in tubs stood at each gun, ready for dousing hot or burning wads, and the lieutenants were inspecting gun positions as their captains reported them manned and ready.

The ship forged on through the lively waters at the entrance to Salcombe harbour, flinging great clouds of foam from either bow. Further from the coast the wind was free of Bolt Head's influence and the sea distinctly calmer, but it suited Pellew's nature to keep the battle in more troubled water.

Aloft, we could see clear across the finger of rocks which had hidden our adversary from deck level. She was well handled in the gusting winds, her bright colours making a brave show streaming out from the mizzen peak.

The *Nymphe* had the advantage of being the weather ship, and Pellew ordered a course to the south-east to cut off the enemy from his home ports. However, it became apparent that nothing was further from the Frenchman's mind than to run away, for he braced hard up to intercept *Nymphe*.

Pellew's eyes narrowed and at his word, the officer of the watch raced aloft with a telescope, bellowing down from the crosstrees that there were no other ships in sight to account for such boldness.

"So, our Frenchman is throwing down the gauntlet is he

– and on our own doorstep – stout fellow," murmured Pellew. "Pray walk round the guns' crews with me, Israel." Israel was Pellew's brother. He was bubbling and lithe like Pellew himself.

The men at the guns paused as the captain took a position amidships.

"Now my lads," he called, "This will be the first action of the war – ship to ship, too, and evenly matched, hey? The whole country will want to hear if we Cornishmen are as good as our fathers on the sea. Remember your gun drill, and when we lay him on board, I promise you shall have your chance with cutlass and pike, for I mean to take this Frog, and earn some prize money for all of us. Good luck, 'Nymphes'!"

He was answered by hasty huzzas for Israel, who was already chiding the crew to their quarters.

Cleopatre's yards were braced hard back to hold her course to windward, and the combined speed of the two ships as they converged had already lessened the gap. The *Nymphe* had now crossed the enemy's bow and her gunners could see her other side broaden out to larboard, glistening with spray.

With more significance they saw a grim line of French gun ports, heeled away from them and opened.

From my position aloft I saw that our own gun ports were heeled, half under water and tight closed. I was then with Yanto amongst the topmen, coiling grappling lines to heave into the French rigging. Around us tense Marines sighted their pieces at the enemy's deck.

Cleopatre's bow was under a cable distant, when *Nymphe* clewed-up the sails on her fore and main, spilling much wind, so that her headway lessened perceptibly. The ship came upright and now her ports could be opened, allowing the guns to fire in successive thunderclaps as each gun bore. But the grey clouds of our smoke was lit by the Frenchman's reply, a broadside.

My heart missed a beat at the rending crash of balls striking us and at the frantic screams of a wounded man. Spare gun captains were moving ready to man the starboard battery.

Nymphe was hardly clear of the enemy's stern before the wheel was put down to start her rapid turn to starboard but, inevitably, she would be to leeward and only the rapid sheeting of her hard braced canvas enabled her to claw back ground in pursuit of the enemy.

Pellew roared orders for three cheers, the much vaunted British 'huzzas' which boosted his crew's temper, at the expense of the Frenchman's. He waved his hat in delight, "By God, he wants to fight!"

The smoke, when it blowed away, revealed *Cleopatre*'s fore royal mast falling through the fore rigging, fouling all as it went, and a cheer went up from our fo'c'stlemen, though it did not discommode the Frenchmen for long, as they cut it clear to bob astern in their wash.

Nymphe's spread of canvas now greatly exceeded the Frogs' and fathom by fathom we crept up on her lee side, being heeled away from her so that our ports were clear of the water and our guns run out, It would be a full broadside this time we figured.

We still carried our higher masts aloft, bearing the royal and topgallant canvas, although it was almost an unheard thing in battle, while the Frenchman had struck his, we observed.

Since the ports on the enemy's engaged side were under water, it was only by taking her canvas off, as we had, that she could come upright and bare the guns. LeBocq, their captain, thought to mask our sails from the wind by closing us. But he was almost stopped and wallowing, while, as our upper canvas towered above his, we kept our way.

To get his guns into action and at the same time remove and re-set his canvas, before we sailed past, would have been a gigantic task

All *Nymphe*'s gun captains had their eyes fixed on Mr Israel, as he balanced near the rail, sword raised, and his gleaming blade flashed down when he judged we were sailing abreast of *Cleopatre*.

A deafening blast smote our ears. Smoke swirled around and we were passing ahead, almost clear, before they could open their gun ports. Only a few balls came into *Nymphe*, but nothing to the great gashes we saw in the enemy's timbers.

The Frenchman recovered well but a swift turn of our wheel soon had him losing ground to leeward of us, as we surged ahead. Now we eased sheets, closing and dropping astern, as the enemy came up with us – slowly this time.

The captain's voice, hard and uncompromising, called out, "Stand by for boarders, larboard." Before there was time to close, however Mr Israel's guns roared out and the second broadside smashed into the Frenchman, whose whole hull quivered and was thrown away from our sides. Looking down I saw her deck filling with men from below. They were milling round as their petty officers divided them into parties. Their numbers seemed to outweigh the *Nymphe*'s men available for boarding, since Frenchmen customarily carried at least a quarter more crew.

"The devils still want to board us, lads!" I shouted hoarsely, reaching for my first grappling iron. Amid all the noise of shot and shouting, the master's voice came through his speaking trumpet.

"Grappling irons away, up top." A score of hooks flew into their rigging. and the grim task of hauling taut began. Slowly, the rolling sides of *Cleopatre* and *Nymphe* closed, pitching and grinding.

It was like clockwork. We scrambled down the disengaged side as marines in the tops joined those mustered on deck to lay a storm of musket and rifle fire over the packed French horde. Without waiting for orders, the marines on deck snatched up their boarding pikes, while their brethren in the tops continued their rifle fire over the enemy decks.

"Mr Brandish," Pellew called, doffing his cocked hat and waving it gracefully towards the enemy's rail. "If you please, sir."

A wave of scarlet flooded over the enemy rail in the wake of Mr Brandish's plump buttocks, the marines, as always, forming the first wave of boarders to reach the enemy's deck.

"Huzza, huzza," they shrieked, lunging their pikes at the Frenchmen. Their momentum pushed the foe back, almost to the opposite side. But more *Cleopatre*'s were scrambling on deck and groping for arms.

Down below, Israel Pellew had selected a few guns for double-shotting, in one last attempt to blow havoc amongst the French guns at point blank range. It was all done 'hanging on a split yarn' for timing and made a bloody shambles; shaking the close-embraced ships.

A lone voice, shouting 'Kernow, Kernow', sparked a mass chorus from Cornish throats, as they lashed their guns to the ship's side. On deck they came into clouds of familiar fumes, grasping for their pikes and cutlasses. The captain would lead his 'jackers', as they called themselves, in the next wave of boarders.

Yanto and I were grabbing for our pikes and cutlasses, when Ned appeared out of the melee on deck.

"Stay close, Mr Davies," he rasped, with wild eyes rolling. "Ain't no banyan this, so keep this young'un covered a'tween us."

With some breathless huzzas we swung over the rail to the Frenchman's deck. Ned slipped momentarily on a streak of blood, but recovered to parry a pass by a French officer who was swallowed up in the maul.

I saw Ned was seized with a wild lust for battle, and sticking to his coat tails, slashing wildly, I felt the same fever. We had glimpses of Captain Pellew, who suddenly turned. His men were being surrounded, and he bellowed into the ear of the beefy marine. "Brandish, kindly break that mob at the main hatch."

Without a word the panting redcoat shrilled his whistle, and pointed. The men on his right formed into a wedge, and charged into the group being rallied by a huge Frenchman in a red cap. They were reinforced by Israel's gunners, a large proportion of whom produced loaded pistols from their waistbands, and scattered Red Cap's men from the hatchway. A small guard was sufficient to pin the Frenchmen below. At Pellew's word Israel sped on board *Nymphe* to muster the last wave of boarders.

The purser was in the forefront, festooned with pistols, and the cook, armed with his razor-sharp carving knives, while the old sailmaker had sent his mates. The gunner's crew had deserted the magazine to join their inimitable captain. The wheel was lashed and idle.

It was a last hope. "Backs to the rail," yelled Ned, using his boots and fists when his cutlass shattered under a blow from an axe.

A French sailor leapt at us, dirk poised, and Yanto

sprang aside, but was unable to avoid a slash from the dirk, and I kneeled to raise my fallen friend.

"No" screamed Ned, chopping at the attacker with the hilt of his cutlass. He swung me to my feet, "Pike forward," he grated, "Yanto 'ull be fine!"

"Bowlin," bellowed Pellew, "Get that lad back on board." He meant me, I believe.

Seeing Ned's doubt, the captain added, "This instant, damn' you. And tell Mr Pellew to fire more guns into their gundeck. The rest of his party to board now, Aah!"

He stumbled as a French sword slashed at his unprotected back. Instinctively I raised my pike in two hands to fend the blow, and, with a jarring ring, the sword shattered on the steel shaft, forcing me again to the deck.

"Urrgh." Relief expelled Pellew's breath. "Get that boy back!" he repeated and plunged back into the fray. Of course, I stood fast…'boy' be damned.

Israel was hasting down the row of his last boarders, slapping their shoulders to make his orders known in that vile din, while Ned pushed pikes into their hands and lined them close to the rail.

A couple of guns exploded below, making an undue crash on *Cleopatre*'s gundeck. The younger Pellew leapt to the rail again, with a great huzza. The last wave followed on his heels, screaming their lungs out.

At this cheer, without reason, a near silence fell on the Frenchman's deck. From below, thin wavering screams rose from the men caught by the last cannonade. At this the ship's captain, Le Bocq, appeared on deck. He raised both hands above his head, his face grey, as he turned from side to side.

"Strike," he cried, and the brave Tricouleur floated slowly to the deck as LeBocq walked below. It was over.

Pellew was exhausted too, but his burdens were not over. He had to tend the sick bay, and console the surgeon in his agony at the toll of dead and wounded. The master and Israel would carry the ship back to Torbay, while the stolid Brandish, the only one to remain unruffled, made the prisoners secure.

Tenders came down Start Bay to discover the cause of gunfire. Pellew refused help from naval vessels. He had not been under the orders of Lord Howe, he said, and only his men would be entitled in claims on the Court of Admiralty.

At this, his popularity increased a hundredfold, while each man – AB or petty officer – would sit down to reckon his prize money.

Pellew was too drained to do much else, but he sent for Ned and myself in his cabin. "Bowlin," he thundered, "I ought to disrate you for putting this lad in the boarding party. What do you say to that?"

"Sir," replied Ned, removing his hat, "With respect to your 'onour, just think how you'd 'a felt if you'd skulked behind at the Saintes or the Moonlight Battle. Now I'll warrant he's a fighter fer the rest of 'is life, sir." He made no mention of the powder boys' part in boarding.

Pellew threw back his head and roared with laughter.

"Young fellow," he said to me, "You saved my life, I do believe, and I give you my hand on it. Bowlin has the right of it. But you will have to do a lot more to earn your ticket for a master's mate. Good luck, sir – and to both of you. I'll put in a word to your flag captain."

Both ships anchored off Dartmouth and repairs were not called off till eight bells, when Pellew declared 'splice the main brace' – in rum.

Only then did the ships fall silent, save for boat's crew

that rowed the guard on their prize. But in the hammocks below men long counted the cost of victory upon their fallen messmates.

Both ships were ordered to Portsmouth for repairs.

We found on arrival that Portsmouth was en fete. Church bells rang and salutes were firing all round as two battered ships entered harbour, piping salutes to senior ships on either side.

The leading frigate, *Cleopatre,* wore the Royal Navy's red ensign superior to the colours of France, and following her was the *Nymphe*, guarding her prize. Boat after cheering boat clustered round the ships, but the crowds fell silent as they saw the number of wounded men bound for Haslar hospital, across the water.

Leave was given as the dockyard took over the ship repairs, and I went with Ned directly to the George to receive a welcome there. Whilst Ned enjoyed the embraces of Doll, his paramour, I was similarly employed in the arms of Rosie, the serving girl, and felt her soft lips on mine. Much drink was consumed by many people in the taproom, and Rosie breathed in my ear. I returned her kisses, ardently as I thought, but, sadly, they raised no feeling of undying love. I fear that Rosie fled with tears on her cheeks. I felt guilty whenever we met afterwards.

Doll was intent on taking me to Eastney to see my mother, but Ned was forcefully opposed to showing the colonel of his regiment that Captain Blunder was possessed of a common seaman in his family.

When the mayor of Portsmouth gave a corporation dinner for the victors of Prawle Point, it was for the officers and men together. I was struck by the change amongst the

Nymphe's youngsters – they indeed bore themselves as men after the battle – men of one ship!

About then came news that my father, Richard Blunder, had bought into a maritime regiment of foot to take service in the West Country, and gazetted as Major.

During dinner in the Guildhall plans were announced to present Captain Pellew with a sword, worth fifty guineas, but we learned that he had been summoned to an audience of the King who was pleased to make him a knight. The hall was rent by cheer after cheer. Thereafter, the toasts were all to 'Sir Edward Pellew', coupled with 'the *Nymphe*'s men.'

The flagship was expected from Torbay, and the crew were given leave till the flagship arrived. And it tempted me to go to Broadwell, until two letters arrived.

The contents of the one from Mistress Golightly hinted of dire news to be imparted only in person. At Torbay she had found the flagship gone. She wrote:

> 'Lord Seckberg has suffered a reverse in his finances and his attorney has advised that he has the right to profits from your holdings, which are under his charge, even of purchasing them for a trifle under the Enclosures Act. Such a hateful business, I do declare. Also there is talk of proceedings for debt against him – oh my dear boy! how put about am I that your ship had sailed. Though I should have made a sorry figure, I fear, for I had quite determined on demanding to see Lord Howe himself.
>
> 'If only I could have been near to console you of such news, for you were always in my heart. Forgive me, dear Andrew. I felt myself so like a

sailor's girl waving 'farewell' to his ship, that I could not stem my weeping.'

My heart thudded, but then I learned that Seckberg had turned away Joe Young, and put one of his bailiffs into my farms. Eleanour Golightly then related her own fortunes. She had left Lady Seckberg, who had sided with her Lord, and she now lived with her sister at a cottage near Nettleton, some mile or two away, taking my grandmother with her.

'I feel it only right that you should be aware of Golightly's departure. The poor troubled man has taken a fowling piece to his head, and I grieve that he was reviled by all for the doing of it at the altar of our church. I cannot say more for I know not what gave rise to such a horrible calumny – may his soul have rest.'

She did say more, however – she is now to be known as Miss Corbett, her former maiden style, and would I please to write to her at her sister's place, which address she gave.

The second letter was my first communication from Joe Young. He thanked me for thinking of him, saying he had little enough of help from Seckberg. He had to take orders from his bailiff, who cared little for livestock or agriculture, but was for ever halooing off to horse races with his Lordship. Joe had had to take his sweetheart to help about the house, while Mistress Golightly seemed to think the old grandmother would be better moved to Nettleton, though presently she fared well enough.

Joe was bitter at his dismissal, but could see it was not the fault of a man run off to sea. He would send an account of his marketing, when his figuring was done, but 'I should not hold out much hope of a fortune, what with the drought and all that.'

On hearing of my news Doll stormed at all she thought responsible for my misfortunes. She had heard of the flagship's return – maybe Ned could procure some leave for me to go to Broadwell.

I fear I had no hopes of leave, but it raised thoughts of just going on the run. However these were dashed to the ground when Ned re-appeared. We were ordered to report on board the *Queen Charlotte*, on the instant.

We were directed to the flag captain's cabin with curious stares, and there found Sir Josiah Probyn, who sat accompanied by a rough-looking man, known to Ned as Jake Hempe, acting bosun of the *Black Joke*. There was also a Mr Jeremy Bashem, known as 'Jemmy', the fourth lieutenant of the flagship.

CHAPTER 9

The flag captain named us, with congratulations on the *Nymphe*'s victory off Prawle Point. He said Sir Josiah had asked that we be present, having peculiar knowledge of Mr Usher and his doings. Mr Bashem was to take command of the *Black Joke*. When he added that Ned and I were to be drafted to the cutter, to join a cutting-out expedition, my mind cleared, and I saw Ned wink.

Captain Hamlet continued, "I believe all here will know that the *Black Joke* was fired on by a vessel they took to be the *Paynton Rose* for whom they were searching. The *Paynton Rose* of course is Lord Howe's despatch vessel and was on a mission, mid-Channel, for Mr Usher to make contact with the frigate force guarding King George at sea. You will understand how embarrassing it'd be if the admiral's own aide and his despatches fall into French hands."

"Sir, your pardon if you please," Mr Bashem broke in, "it is common knowledge that the damned *Paynton Rose* has been sighted in harbour."

Captain Hamlet admitted with a resigned smile that it was damned likely, and closed discussion by saying Mr Bashem had outlined a splendid plan which he would explain to his crew directly on getting under way. "Tell all your hands that Black Dick wishes them Godspeed."

We sailed within an hour, heaving to off the Nab for Lieutenant Bashem to read his appointment in command, choking down our laughter, for he was dressed in a woollen smock, smelling liberally of fish, as we all were. We saw, however, that it was Jemmy's big moment. Our aim was to cut out the *Paynton Rose* and rescue Mr Usher and her crew. We were bound for the Breton port of l' Aberwrac'h.

The cook served thick stew of fish, with leeks and other vegetables, typical fare of small ships, and by the start of the morning watch, when we were called, it was to shoot our nets and cruise ever nearer the coast of France under fishing lights. The *Black Joke* could not be rated either as a 'sloop', or 'yacht', for she did not fit any of these titles. Now she looked like many another fisher craft going about her business around us, though we had no fish hold and only took enough of the haul to fill the cook's kettles.

Hempe and Ned had shared the watch through the night, astonished to find their skipper was awake too, insisting on getting the feel of the ship, and, most of all, brimming with plans for preparing the vessel and her crew for storming the enemy's coast to retrieve what was 'ours.'

Mr Probyn, as he was known on board, had arrived with a young AB, named Tregorrick, drafted from Falmouth. He had been introduced to the crew as having a rare talent – that of speaking the old tongue of Cornwall.

"Now Cornish is akin to Breton, and the folk over there," he waved his hand toward the coast, "can also understand Cornish, lads. Now he's my tutor. Don't disturb yourselves – Tregorrick speaks English perfectly well and will accept an offer of a tot in either tongue."

He did not add that a Breton-speaker would help immensely his mission to assess the strength of the French fleet in Brest Harbour.

As the day ripened, the hands worked below a screen of spare nets, where they prepared the boats for the attack, muffling the rowlocks and oars, stowing sharpened arms. Mr Hempe sailed the *Black Joke* closer and closer to the north of rock-bound islets which masked L'Aberwrac'h.

Bashem was aloft scanning the winding passages that led to the little port. At last an image swam briefly into the lenses of his telescope and settled on a fishing cutter with a pattern of sailcloths, white and brown, that convinced us that it was the *Paynton Rose*.

She was alongside the small quay of L'Aberwrac'h, and he slid down to deck to plot a course through the uncertain marks and currents.

Come dinner at noon, most of the arms had been stowed in the boats, and a vicious one-pounder fitted in the bows of the lead boat, with priming powder and charges of grape. The second boat was to follow us, and tow the first back to the *Black Joke* after landing the cutting out party.

A tense air now settled over the ship as the day wore on, while Hempe stolidly took command of the *Black Joke*, stiff-faced, for he had thought to lead the expedition himself.

Bashem timed our departure till after moonset having determined a favourable tide after low water, when the two boats were manned and cast off. Now Jemmy's drilling of the boat party for them to accustom themselves in manning their thwarts on a dark night gave proof of success.

I had to crouch behind the gun in the bows, trailing a long rod to take soundings while Jemmy steered aft. He had one chance to succeed in this hasty descent on the French coast, yet inwardly he exulted in the task.

In my place in the bows I peered ahead seeing only blacker objects above water level and lighter flashes in the water itself. The stroke of the oarsmen was deliberate and slow, and I took comfort from the thought that our difficulties would also apply to enemy watchers.

A voice aft whispered, "Gaff cutter, right ahead sir," and we boated oars, save one of the stroke oars, who used his blade to punt us silently to the dark mass before the bows.

The boat astern closed us quietly, the crew grasping our gunnels as they came abreast. With muffled cutlasses, the first crew swarmed on deck over the taffrail. Still the silence reigned.

There were faint gleams of starlight when a fitful breeze shifted the clouds, and from my position as after lookout saw shadowy outlines of the village. It was barely four cables to the nearest house. The faintest of lights showed in one building only, that I took to be an inn, by its size.

Those searching the ship below decks appeared like shadows to whisper that they had not found anyone on board.

"Our quarry Usher could be anywhere from Brest to Paris, be he a prisoner of the French or no," muttered Bashem ruefully.

His disappointment was felt by all of us, for there was no relish in the prospect of lying in wait for three nights in an enemy harbour.

We landed Sir Josiah and AB Tregorrick on what appeared to be the town quay, where they melted into the darkness about their own devices to reconnoitre the state of readiness of the French ships in port at Brest.

Both boats then rowed to a point opposite the channel by which we came in. There the stores carried in the second boat were put ashore on a disused slip covered in debris and broken boats. Weeds and saplings grew up through the piles of nets and fishing buoys, almost covering them.

The one inch boat's gun was landed from the lead boat which was taken in tow to return to the *Black Joke* before sunrise. We prayed they would meet no mishap, or we would be marooned in enemy territory, and probably taken as spies, to meet our doom under the guillotine.

Among the gear landed was an old sheet of canvas, covered with dirt and patches of rust. With this and two elderly oars we rigged a shelter in a large ship's cutter that lay there, her back broken and sides cracked open.

It was to be our new home for three days, and all hands gathered to make it more shipshape. In the bows we rigged the large telescope and the boat's gun, both peering from under the canvas, and draped with weeds.

A sheltered fire was lit to steam a hash of pork and ship's biscuit, and some sleep taken before the sun came up and the marauding rats retired to their holes.

When Lieutenant Bashem returned with three of his men they pronounced the village almost clear of inhabitants, and after a meal retired to stretch out on the cleaner canvas I had spread. It was time for my relief but I stayed, clearing away mess traps to be scrubbed by the forenoon watchmen

At first light I was called and took my place at the telescope. To my amazement I saw a single mounted man, dressed in a red and blue coat. I awakened Mr Bashem at once, to come to the telescope.

"French cavalry, I think, is he the only one?" I could not say 'aye' or 'nay' but a pair of peasant women arrived whom we assumed to be inn servants living in the village. The trooper led his mount to the back. In a few moments he appeared at the door from inside, and let them in.

When smoke appeared at the chimneys, we took it to confirm that the inn contained but three persons.

More arrived later, however, with cartloads of timber and soon amidst much hammering and shouting, they reared what seemed to be a double gibbet, on which we kept a fascinated watch and saw it transformed into a dreaded guillotine.

Much later we pieced together the ominous mishaps that befell our comrades on the road to Brest. Probyn and Tregorrick had been eating dried biscuit when the sound of hooves reached them. It was before sunrise but the sky was light high on the hills where the Brest road ran to the west. They had quickly retired behind a thicket of gorse, their pistols drawn, as three horseman passed towards L'Aberwrac'h.

As Probyn related, disaster struck when Tregorrick failed to hide his pistol after the three horsemen had passed. A voice suddenly boomed, "Hola, Messieurs, ça va? Un bon matin, n'est ce pas?"

Tregorrick's hand flew to snatch up the pistol, which lay on the grass before him, and turning as he did, saw a fourth horseman, sighting a huge pistol at his head. The AB stayed his hand in fright as the new arrival emitted a piercing whistle which caused the party ahead to return at the gallop.

At this prospect, Probyn relates, he was sick with himself for leading such a raw hand into danger. He had not heard the fourth man's approach, for he came on them, not on the track, but riding over thick, soft turf. He was even more resigned when he recognised Usher, the flag lieutenant, with his wolf-like grin, but neither man acknowledged the other.

Adopting a rough form of Norman French, Probyn pleaded that they did no wrong. They had heard there were some old fishing boats at L'Aberwrac'h, and sought the prospect of their patron buying one, as all their boats had gone to the privateering trade at St Malo, alas.

As spokesman, Usher indicated the Cornish lad's pistol, and invited Probyn to submit to being tied up, which was quickly effected. The intelligence chief was able to drop his stock of money in long grass, and sought to warn Tregorrick what their story should be, but the lad was clubbed senseless and flung over a horse, while the fourth horseman was ordered back to Brest to summon extra troopers.

The party resumed its journey to L'Aberwrac'h with their prisoners. The little port was still dark when the two naval men were flung into separate rooms at the inn.

Eventually it was possible to assemble what came next. We learned from Tregorrick that he was awakened by water from a pail dashed over his face.

In pain he struggled up, but was held facing a blank wall. Someone he could not see was holding his shoulders, and as his mind cleared he sensed there were others in the room.

"He says to me, 'Easy my 'andsome, all's well – don't 'ee struggle now, I'll get ye up.' I'll swear it was a Devon voice. He calls fer a tot of rum for me, but afore it come, I asks a question – 'Where am I?' says I.

"'Tis L'Aberwrac'h, my friend, don't 'ee remember where you come ashore?' He turns to his mate. 'Oh aye', says I. 'Only two more nights till Mr Bashem comes for us'. He drops me flat. I reckon I seen him before, a tall dark party, black patch on 'is eye and a red wool 'at. He asks me where would my friends be now. But of a sudden I remembers Mr Probyn and wouldn't say more. 'Voilá, mes enfants, we 'ave learned enough, hien?' says another voice and I sees it is this Usher speaking in the Breton-French. He turns to his mate. 'Monsieur Bashem is fourth in the English flagship and seeks to take the *Paynton Rose* from us, but whether he comes from the sea or is here in hiding, we shall surprise him.' "

The cutting out party led by Lieutenant Bashem spent all that day under cover, arming themselves with pistol and cutlass and eating a meal of lobscouse, cold, until sunset when they were ordered to the slipway to stretch their limbs. I watched as their shadowy forms faded into the dark.

Once alongside the *Paynton Rose*, it was simple to reach the deck by a boarding ladder, and the entire party was on deck in seconds. Following the orders given that afternoon, they took station below deck, creeping down in darkness, till Bashem lit the lantern, and caused all to blink at its sudden light.

At this moment the boarding party saw three troopers with their backs pressed to the ship's side, presenting their pistols. A mocking voice addressed the boarders in English.

"Gentlemen, I beg of you – let us have no troublesome bloodshed today. I assure you that my men surround you in every compartment. Ah, I see that you intend to be sensible. Good, we will depart to the village inn, my friends, where we hold some more of your compatriots."

Lieutenant Bashem started at what he recognised as Usher's voice; the villain was with the enemy. He had no course other than to surrender in ignominy, and so they marched under the guns of the cavalrymen, and were held under lock and key by ruthless enemies in the inn.

Seeing the shadowy outline of the guillotine, Bashem confessed his dread that, due to his failures, his crew were bound for the almost certain fate meted out to spies.

At the boat slip, a flurry of seabirds' wings had wakened me to the realisation that I was alone. I took to the telescope at almost feverish intervals, but hearing nothing and seeing less, I divined a disaster. That my shipmates had failed was almost certain.

Miserably, I manned the telescope again. Through the bushes there were glimpses of movement and smoke rose from the inn. I must figure a way to get nearer, using my poacher's skills. As there was no hope of help from the *Black Joke*, I had to release my friends single-handed.

Before the inn the thickets appeared to be dense, but doubtless there would be sentries to evade – or kill. My eye then fell on the boat's gun, and I decided to set up a firing post as soon as darkness fell. Perhaps there was a chance that I could get word to the prisoners, and smuggle weapons to them.

It was essential to take a meal. There was little time to trap water fowl or catch the fish that abounded there – hard tack and water would suffice. Several journeys would be needed to mount the gun, to plot the sentries' movements and smuggle arms to my mates.

A track made by small animals seemed ideal, and I was able to conceal myself all the way, and set up the small telescope before the inn door. There was activity round the guillotine for some hours, then the workmen trooped inside to join what appeared to be revelry, which I guessed to come from the left side of the inn. A sentry idled near the door, exchanging banter with those inside.

It took four more journeys to move the arms – pikes, tight bound with pistols and cutlasses in sacks, and lashed to my back. After sunset, the gun, its grape and powder were got in position with much exertion.

I needed a rest, some food and weak grog, before undertaking my last venture of that night, which was to talk to my shipmates. For this I arrived a little before the carousing died down.

Sure, there was a new sentry to go rounds of the building. Once it was all quiet, I found his tours to take but five minutes, twice in the hour. After each round he sat on his heels, smoking, with his fusil propped nearby.

I must take the first opportunity, for who knew how long it took to extricate myself. It was but a minute to reach the building's right hand side, and follow in his wake.

I could hear him trundle ahead, vanishing to the rear. A stout timber was set on the right hand side, its base against the wall and sloped outward to a pile of stone. Likely it had served as a shore to the next cottage, now a ruin. Barred openings were alongside, high in the inn wall. As I ducked to pass below the shore, I heard a low voice.

"Damned if a smart ship's boy 'ouldn't come in handy, Mr Bashem!" I knew it at once for Ned's, sounding as imperturbable as ever, and my heart leapt.

"Damned uncivil to keep us tied up, without a knife, between us, sir," – and I passed my own knife through the bars, where it was taken by someone tied at the wrists.

Quickly I glanced over the ruins next door and saw that they gave ample cover behind the fallen stones and waist high weeds. Lightly, I jumped amongst them and hid for three of the sentry's rounds. I needed time to inform Ned of my proposals in the fewest words.

The sentry came round, humming a tune and knocking the butt of his weapon on the wall. He was old and doddery and a catch came to my throat as I pondered my next move – to kill him or his relief. He passed and I clambered up the timber shore.

"Chief," I whispered, "back in one hour."

Then I ran, reaching the gun's site direct from the ruined cottage. An hour passed, during which time I wrestled with my conscience over what I planned to do, while my fingers twisted the means. Back at the wooden shore, Ned had waited silently.

"Ned, I must kill the sentry," I began, "I have made a rabbit snare, big enough to slip round his neck. As he stoops below this timber – it needs a sudden jerk before he can make a sound."

I began to pass the sacks of weapons between the bars, knowing that I must return to the boat slip at once for chippy's tools to loosen the bars. Ned nodded, "Understand, mate. Go to it." Then I fled.

The following night we waited till all had quietened down. The morrow would bring a fiesta for the villagers to attend, a mass execution and there was a certain anxiety amongst us not to be the centre of such a spectacle that would bring us as much anguish as to the villagers doing without it.

As to the breakout, if I was to play a central role, it was not to be so violent as I had feared, for Mr Bashem had amended the plot to strangle the guard, as being too barbaric. I was much relieved as I had feared the taint of murder that should attend me, I was certain, to my dying day. Yet he had to be silenced in a trice, so that no alarm should pass his lips. Had I failed in this, my mess mates would never have escaped the guillotine. A clout on the head from the shadow of the timber strut would suffice, Mr Bashem ruled, since a breakout was to be achieved before he recovered

With a bounding heart, I duly clouted the new sentry, a peasant lad by the look of him, bound and gagged him, then helped remove the loosened bars. We were ready for a set-to.

But first Bashem and Ned crept in at the central window on the rear wall where they stunned and bound the sleeping forms of Usher and Rabouillet, taking Usher with us to the *Paynton Rose*.

With this capture our mission was complete and the C-in-C's aide irrevocably exposed as a Frenchman and a spy.

Under our heavy burdens we filed past the shadowy site of the guillotine, which was designed so soon to embrace us, and I shuddered in the darkness.

On arrival at the *Paynton Rose*, our immediate task was to let go the mooring warps and make sail to our rendezvous with the *Black Joke*.

Taking over the deck of an unfamiliar ship by night was easier than I had feared, for the plan of her rigging was the same in all ships of her sort, but the winding channel we had to negotiate tested even Jemmy, who had planned it for the time the tide was in our favour.

Mr Hempe and the *Black Joke* were there at the appointed hour for our rendezvous.

Once in the open Channel, we were in the domain of the Royal Navy, our greatest haul being to have Usher in bonds. Sir Josiah was saved, though, and his simple Cornishman, although they never reached Brest. At last, with *Black Joke* in company, we set course for home.

CHAPTER 10

When we entered Portsmouth Harbour I had visions of a meeting with Eleanour, but, of course, it was beyond reason that she would pay a second visit after the failure of the first, and I resigned myself to disappointment for she would be unaware of the *Queen Charlotte*'s presence here.

We said farewell to the crews of the *Black Joke* and the *Paynton Rose*, and took our seabags to the flagship. Jemmy Bashem was markedly expansive, and Mr Hempe beamed at the prospect of commanding his old ship.

Ned described the whole action as a 'good run ashore.'

In my mess, I was besieged with questions of our absence, and the whereabouts of my 'winger', Yanto. But they faded on hearing that he had lost a leg at Prawle Point.

Ned and I were summoned to the cabin, to find Captain Hamlet seated with Mr Bashem at his table, two papers lying before them.

"This is Mr Bashem's report of your conduct ashore, Miller. It seems you saved the day there for the whole crew – we owe you a great deal. Take my hand on it and the admiral's compliments, sir. He wishes to see you and Bowlin – and you may expect nothing less than congratulations for your assistance to Sir Josiah Probyn."

His secretary poured wine, while Mr Bashem looked relieved to be in favour, despite his party's capture.

The captain was expansive too, adding that, of course, the safety of His Majesty at sea was our principal concern. Usher was confined on board, he told us, soon to be moved to a prison hulk, the commander-in-chief having agreed not to insist on an early court martial for the scoundrel.

Legal wrangling would cause delay to his further questioning, there being doubts now of his ever having a naval rank or being subject to a court martial.

The second paper on the flag captain's desk was accompanied by a package, which he presented to me. I saw it contained a fine looking dirk, as carried by midshipmen of the fleet, its leather scabbard chased with silver.

It came from Sir Edward Pellew 'for saving his life', said the flag captain – "a service any captain might value," He wrung my hand once more. "Moreover Sir Edward commended you for advancement to able seaman."

Thereupon, red with surprise, I was rated immediately.

Portsmouth Harbour lay cold and cloaked in thick mist, come dawn, but at mid-morning a furore was set up at the finding of a small boat floating near the Sally Port. It was towed to the *Queen Charlotte*, whose boat it was, and contained the bodies of a corporal of marines, shot at close range and of two ABs beaten to death horribly. At dawn these three had been rowing an inmate of the ship's cells to the tender of the prison hulk. Now the prisoner was gone.

Once more Ned and I were before the captain, as were others, including the first lieutenant, and a call went to Sir Josiah Probyn, in his rooms at the Keppel's Head, near the dockyard gate. The missing prisoner was Usher.

The uproar spread wide. It seemed that he would have landed on the quay at Old Portsmouth. Ned and I were told to search where he might have taken refuge amongst the crowded stews or brothels in the slums away from the main thoroughfares. Sir Josiah knew of my connection with Usher at the George, another place for enquiry, while help was requested of the county law officers.

In the George Inn's taproom, Doll suggested "trying that gypsy girl at No. 92," Hellfire Betsy's establishment.

"Jenny!" I exclaimed, and Doll rolled her eyes archly at me, while Ned smacked his thighs, laughing at my expression. "Usher went with her," I retorted hotly.

Without further ado I slipped away to No. 92.

The madam was chary of anyone she deemed unsuitable, and stared at me with hostility when, with beating heart, I asked for Jenny. At that, I saw that Betsy recognised me.

"La, young fellow, have you the lucre fer such company? Ain't you on the young side to throw away a sailors' pay at those games?" She paused, eyes like gimlets.

"She ain't 'ere, and I can't tell where she is – Lawks! ain't you the lad wot saved Sir Edward in that battle?"

Unthinking, I nodded, and she grasped me to her voluminous bosom, plastering sticky kisses over my face.

"Ha, I do declare you wants 'er so's you may act the 'ero – well Jenny's too damned partick'lar fer that, my lad."

"Oh, no, we're trying to trace the naval gentleman, and think he may be with her." It was the wrong tack to take.

"Wot's 'e done?" Betsy's voice was hard as flint.

I thought quickly. The wave of patriotic feeling that swept over Pompey wouldn't prevent Betsy from siding with an underdog and former client. She wouldn't swallow a tale that one of my age was on the King's business, either.

"I am sent by a brother officer of his ma'am. He is wanted as second in an affair of honour. Miss Jenny knows of it, I believe, ma'am." I kept a straight face.

"Ho yes, young 'ero. Huh! likely she's taken 'im to 'er own place, rot 'er, but seeing as it's you, I'll tell you 'ow to get there and mind you tells 'er she's wanted 'ere fer business. Why any gennulman 'ould want to go to that stinking sty of hers... ah!"

She threw up her hands in mock despair. I sped away with her directions.

The alley I entered was stinking indeed, and almost pitch black. Squelching noises in the puddles told me there were others about – I felt their eyes upon me. At last I came to a dimly-seen farthing dip, whose flickering light, guttering at the edge of a bench, revealed what appeared to be an old crone, touting for trade – though whether for herself or others, she did not appear to know.

She accosted me in a maudlin way, under a cloud of hashish and gin smells, and, as I closed with the door, I saw its number was as given by Hellfire Betsy.

"Is Jenny in?" was all I asked, but she set up a series of wild shrieks and garbled mouthings, so that I assumed Jenny was in and turned to mount the stairs to a flood of tears. "Jenny, oh why is it allus Jenny," followed by vile curses.

All at once there was a rush, and I was seized, I sensed, by three pairs of hands. All my attackers spoke in French, but since my head was banged against the walls, I may have lost my senses. I awoke to find myself being thrown through a door to land on a heap of blankets.

With an effort I eased open my eyes, in time to see a solitary unkempt form leaping at me and with a knife poised high, aimed at my neck.

I gasped as I rolled away. Luckily it was downhill from the summit of the blanket mound, and I knew that I must do something urgently – for my very life.

The knife plunged into the blankets, inches from my neck and my attacker, came at me again. While I tried to clear away the tangle of blankets, he was snarling with rage.

It was Usher.

He wrenched his knife out, and, crawling groggily over the bed, raised the weapon for a final blow. A piercing scream rose,

"Naow, no!"

Twisting and spitting, a lithe figure appeared as if by magic from the tumbled bedclothes and flung itself on Usher, kneeing and clawing with all four limbs. It was Jenny, as darkly naked as the day she was born.

The knife flew away again, jolting heavily against my arm as it went. The trampling melee made the soft mattress heave like short seas across a shoal bank, and I could not see the knife amongst the flying feet.

Jenny, however, scooped it up, squealing like a stuck pig as she lunged in a highly professional way towards Usher's head. She had been used to knife fights from an early age in many gypsy camps, and at last Usher, who had banged his head against an iron door lock, subsided, scratched and bleeding.

Jenny turned a dazzling smile on me, her shapely breasts swinging so that I goggled and blushed and gazed away.

"There sir," she laughed mockingly, "Do you pass a poor gypsy girl her petticoat, pray. For I be too modest to stand before a lusty sailor in my bare buff."

She broke into peals of laughter as she pulled wide gypsy skirts upon brown legs and wriggled into her skimpy blouses, her knife never far from Usher's belly.

She addressed him. "Now my fine lover, you would spit this young bantam all over my bed – yes?".

He shook his head to clear it. Being on the run, he had formed a contract with the gypsies, and relied on the Romany bond. "Believe me, Jen, he's an enemy, sent to drag me back for court martial, as I told you".

"Since when did the King's Navy send babes the likes of him to catch a fine bucko, like you?" demanded Jenny. "A blood feud I may understand but not with a young cockerel like this?"

"He's from my ship – what was I to think?" cried Usher, his guile returning with his wits.

Jenny looked hard into my eyes, and winked slowly. After the fashion of the Romanies, she had read the truth of Usher's claim in my face.

To Usher she said, "Well, you are a handsome client and I've taken your gold. I will keep to our bargain and see you safe to the Romney men of the marshes, but I'll not trade your escape to France for this young'un's life. If you harm a hair on 'is head, your number's up, savvy?"

Usher climbed to his feet. "Enough, it is nearly light."

"Naow," hissed Jenny. "We cannot leave him here for Dipsy Dora to find – she'll make a hue and cry all over Portsmouth. He must come to the camp, till you're clear."

She pulled on a pair of red leather boots, and slipped the long knife into the right one. "Now lovers, we must all dress the part. Lord, this is better than the playhouse."

The still-dazed Usher was clothed in a gypsy jacket, a coloured shirt and a battered cloak, but, even under a floppy brimmed hat, Jenny was not satisfied. She rubbed his face liberally with a dark juice, flirting all the while with me, whom she called 'your honour', or 'my lover.'

She bent over me, her dark curls brushing my face, which she covered in moist, lingering kisses, that caused me to tremble deliciously and blush deep red. Jenny was delighted at the havoc she caused me. With Usher's help, I was bound lightly at the wrists and ankles and rolled in an old carpet.

"Do not grieve, great lord, we go to a Romany camp.

But now you must be our prisoner. Be still for a while for I cannot wait to kiss you," She slipped a gag into my mouth, "for fear you break into a sea shanty, sweetheart."

The donkey cart was outside, into which my carpet roll was pitched with several others, whilst Jenny sat, legs trailing, and spoke to the animal in the Romany tongue to start him on our journey.

There was sparse traffic on our route, but the London coach, arriving at the road barrier, distracted the guards when we were stopped. It proved a cursory halt, and we were waved on.

Fortunately, I was released after miles of jolting, half-stifled, and sweating from my confinement in one position, my arm was crushed and throbbing.

At dawn we arrived at a large common, covered with gypsy vans, whose scattered campfires emitted a curtain of smoke that mingled with a thin mist off the sea. We moved on to a small Hall at Funtington, whose meadow accommodated several caravans of clan chiefs.

They included Jenny's father, Ruben Forward, and she sprang up the steps to greet him, disappearing through a curtain. Caleb, the family guard dog, came to act as my sentry once he had thoroughly sampled my scent.

There was no sign of Usher, but a brawny youth of about twenty years, scrutinised me too, from a position sprawled idly on the ground. He was Bruno Forward and he so resembled Jenny that I guessed he was her brother. He just nodded.

Jenny came to say that I was welcome and took me into the gleaming van where old man Forward sat, swathed in a blanket amidst a fortune's worth of garish pottery.

The meeting, brief though it proved to be, was a symbol of the clan's protection, henceforth. The old patriarch put aside the tube of a strange smoking pipe and rose to embrace me. That done, he wandered outside to acquaint the other chiefs, of my arrival.

Jenny's family and I fed on a fine meal of stewed rabbits, basted in herbs and a sweet-tasting wine, until my aches began to ease in a warm glow. Outside there was a mass exodus towards the common, where booths and kiosks were springing to life, with a promise of the main events – horse racing and prize fights. Drowsily I heard the hubbub of growing crowds arriving, amidst shouts and hammering. I dreamed that I was alarmed by a menacing crescendo of barking from Caleb, but when I crawled out of my berth there was no sign, but a moving shadow and the dog had calmed down.

Caleb gave a little whine of welcome later when Jenny returned and I woke with a fiery face, but when I threw back the blanket, my teeth chattered with cold and my head thundered.

At once Jenny pronounced that I had taken a fever. She pulled up my sleeve to reveal a long weal, a wound that ran from shoulder to below the elbow. It was just where Usher's knife had struck me. She dressed it with a herb poultice, and lay me back murmuring softly.

Later when I awoke, it was dark. I felt better except for a sweat, and, like a ghost, my nurse came to see me with potions to drink. She felt my hot forehead.

"Hoi, gorgio, you are over-dressed," she whispered, using the Romany word for someone who is not of gypsy blood, and began to strip me of my clothes. At first I was too weak to feel the indignity of it. Her hands on my burning flesh were everywhere, cool and soft, and I was sure her lips helped too.

She whispered in my ear and I felt her naked body

move against me, her hands everywhere, and her legs circling my unresisting form. All that happened after that is lost, for my imagination was drowned in a sultry dream.

By morning I had recovered, to find myself alone in the van, save for the snoring Caleb. But the dream stayed with me in my hazy state all that day.

The events of that day, the prize fight, the roaring crowd and the belt awarded to Bruno Forward as new champion, all swam past me, till I realised the vast crowds were running away. Lookouts had proclaimed the approach of mounted troopers come to disperse the illegal gathering.

It became more a carnival than a rout. Elated and mirthful, the crowd generated a mass spirit of jollity in flight, knowing the impossibility of the small troop to act against such numbers. The troopers knew it too, and advanced steadily, at a jog trot, at least four fields distant. All seemed a laughable lottery, for the troopers bided their time to make a token snatch or two.

The Romanies were departing en masse, Bruno amongst them, but Jenny was not with them. A huge man forced his way to my side. It was one of Bruno's seconds, who slapped my back jovially, and thrust a packet into my hands.

"That way, gorgio – she has gone away," he boomed, and, blindly, I pushed in the direction he pointed.

A band of drunken tars had been betting on the fight, but they were cables away, and running in the opposite direction. I realised I had to get back to the *Queen Charlotte*.

The heaving mass showed no sign of Jenny's donkey cart, and I paused at the sight of the four-horse carriage belonging to Lady Letty, the wife of our admiral, Earl Howe. She was notorious for driving, clad in men's clothes, to sporting galas like this, and for her appetite for handsome prize fighters. The wheels of her carriage had sunk in the soft turf, and willing hands, laughing and shouting, flocked round to put their shoulders at her disposal.

Wondering about Bruno's whereabouts caused me to regard the stampeding crowd more closely, when a face swam into view. It was Usher's once more.

He was at the other side of Lady Letty's coach, just above the surging crowd, and I realised that he sat a pie pony of the gypsies. His eyes were on me, his arm raised and a streak of light traced the path of his knife through the air. The knife thudded into the coach.

His lips parted in a snarl, and he lashed at the crowd with his crop for pushing his pony and spoiling his aim. No-one noticed. All around the gentry were lashing their way through the masses.

There were huzzas and shouts of "Go to it m'lady," "Whip up, Letty," and bawdy cries of support as her coach got moving. Her long whip slashed and cracked as the wheels began to turn and the coach to lurch forward.

By now Usher had cleared a space around his pony and stood in the stirrups, raising another knife. His throwing arm moved back. But before he could launch it, his face dissolved in blood under the lash of the whip flicked backwards by Lady Letty. Unbalanced, he fell to the ground. Lady Letty waved the whip in my direction, laughing at me conspiratorially, while the crowd swarmed to assist the blinded horseman who screamed on the turf.

I ran on, panting, in a confusion of faces and folk, and the cavalry cantering, good humouredly, in the rear.

In my heart I felt that life ahead lay cold and empty, though perhaps there lay a shred of hope in Hellfire Betsy's. It was in the same direction as the flagship.

CHAPTER 11

By chance the way was uphill now, and pausing for breath, I saw streams of people still pouring astern of me.

It could not be known for certain whether Usher was among them, but he would be dismounted at least, for a skein of bright-clad Romanies was threading through the crowds, in chase of a pretty pie pony, running loose.

I marked a fork in the road to my left and took it, seeing no others turn that way. It soon became a steep farm track and, cursing myself for a booby, I turned about, only to find that a gentleman's coach had turned into the lane behind me. I hid myself in bushes.

The coach swayed and banged over the rough ground until it rounded a bend just beyond my hiding place. Both horses reared and snorted as they came to a halt, amidst a torrent of curses from coachman and passengers alike.

"What's afoot Jenkins? The dragoons ain't taken us, have they?"

"Tree, yer 'onour! Clear across this damn lane." The coachman resumed his cursing, the gist being that he resented being ordered to drive up this bloody goat track, and how long the axles would stand such dam fool ruts and rocks. Bloody lunatics!

"Nay nay, Jenkins, 'twon't do for a Justice of the Peace to be taken by the damn dragoons. Get on with it, man!"

Another head appeared at the window. "Where are we? Let me drive if that damn Jenkins ain't up to it. Hey, I swear this bottle's empty." The offending flagon described an arc and came straight for me.

Alarmed, I sprang from cover, and all three in the coach

screeched at the sight. The two inside disappeared from view, and Jenkins hollered and fumbled for his whip.

"Ah, 'tis only a lad, a sailor lad," he roared in relief. "Hey you, lad, shift that branch, clear the way. Sharp about it now, or I'll put this whip about you."

I tugged at the awkward branch.

"Who's there, Jenkins; what's that lad?"

"It's naught but a lad, a sailor lad, Sir John."

"What the devil is he at?"

Jenkins muttered in a carrying voice, "What's it look like, silly old fool." He shouted more loudly "Shifting the bloody tree, Sir John – this bloody lane be damnation clogged, if you bloody please... ah chocker, that is – it's bloody choked. Coach won't take it, sir; the 'osses won't take it, and I be damned if I'll take it. Aargh!" He seemed to think his meaning clear and spat in disgust.

"I can't shift this branch," said I, gasping.

"Whoa, who's that? Footpads? Where's my pistol, dammit?"

The second head appeared again, and I began to laugh at the sight of three elderly men, all gawping at me. All three of them were drunk, including the coachman, who was now dithering round at the horses' heads in the dusk.

"The dragoons have passed, sir," I offered.

"Hey, what's that?"

"Went by ten minutes ago. It's safe on the highway."

"Ha, then do you give Jenkins a hand to turn her round, and you shall have a ride for your trouble." The head disappeared inside.

"Here's another bottle, Sir John; what are they at?"

I stopped dead. The gentleman in the grey wig seemed familiar.

Suddenly, certainty struck – it was Blunder, of course,

Sir John Blunder, my own grandfather, whose son was the start of all my misfortunes. I was too tired to reason.

Jenkins succeeded in steering the coach to Portsmouth and we inmates awoke to find ourselves alongside of the *Queen Charlotte* without further mishap. By this time Squire Blunder had tumbled to the fact that I was Andrew Miller, his own grandson, at first doubting that it was welcome news.

He had come to Hampshire in search of his son, only to find that Richard Blunder was posted to Plymouth, where, as major in a regiment of foot, he was to embark with his company for duty as marines. The old man had encountered my mother at Eastney and inspected his baby grandson, before succumbing to the temptation of a race meeting added to a prize fight for the championship of several counties.

I gathered that the arrival of the cavalry and the chase from the scene only added spice to the occasion, suitable for raising astonishment and envy amongst his cronies at home. Moreover, the finding of a wounded sailor, whom he had rescued from the dragoons, would top all when he announced that the gallant lad was his first grandson.

The bluster he made with the gangway staff, his demands for a doctor's attention and his repeated assertions that he was a 'justice', brought the officer of the day to the gangway. To my dismay Lieutenant Bashem ordered my arrest for having run. He would question me himself, he said, and I was escorted to his cabin on the main deck aft.

Bashem quickly set my mind at rest and, while we waited for the surgeon and Ned Bowlin to arrive, he took pains to explain.

"Your messmates were seething with curiosity at your absence, attended by your previous excursions from the ship – damned jealousy, if you ask me. It wouldn't serve for you to appear on the mess deck, my lad, would it? You'd be unable to satisfy 'em – and they're a damned nosey lot, eh?"

He stuck his head through the canvas 'door', and bellowed for the duty servant. Ned and a Surgeon's Mate had arrived, and in no time my sliced arm was exposed for the latter's inspection. At that moment the wardroom servant arrived, and turned white at the sight.

The youngster overheard the verdict of the surgeon's mate that I would need to be messed in the sick bay, before he was dispatched for a bottle of blackstrap and some hot water and sugar.

"That'll be round the ship by both watches, in the morning," the lieutenant grinned. "Now – only one question; do you know where Usher is?"

I shook my head, "Last seen at Funtington, heading for the Romney Marsh men, sir. He was making off with a horse, stolen from his guides, but was wounded in the eye, maybe both eyes. He was on foot then. I'm certain he'll be found by his pursuers." I refrained from making mention of the gypsies.

At Bashem's instruction, a runner was sent to Sir Josiah's lodging with this information, while Ned brought up my hammock to the sick mess, where I fell asleep and cast aside all my worries about Usher and about Sir John, but not about Jenny, whose ghost followed me down into the corridors of sleep. There I swear I dreamed with a sad smile on my face.

Always, at the back of my mind, I was haunted by the fate of the farms, and the disturbance of wars.

Early the next morning, Ned came to the sick bay and drew me on one side. "You can't work aloft with an arm in that shape, matey. They're sending you to hospital for some fancy sail maker's work on your fin. You'll find it a soft berth, lad."

He winked as he said it, but added, "and take some shore-going gear. Jolly boat in an hour, alongside the south quay. A pass is at the gangway."

And he disappeared.

I knew better than to question Ned Bowlin's guarded orders and presented myself at the gangway with my arm in a sling, for which I found scarcely a need.

So I came to sample the dull life of a hospital patient across the harbour. The stitching was a painful interlude, but, to my good fortune, the wound was on the left arm, and I was left free to write to Eleanour.

Now it dawned that my motives were mixed, for I had formed an attachment with another lady, and felt abashed to think of renewing my correspondence with the Mistress Golightly, or 'Miss Corbett', as she now styled. herself. These doubts flew however, when a familiar voice hailed me.

Stumping on sticks into the mess room there came Yanto, beaming in spite of his laboured breathing. He slapped my back and, setting down a canvas wallet, took a seat beside me.

"Welcome to my country seat, shipmate," he grunted, waving at the whitewashed walls around us and the small high windows. "I heard on the scuttle-butt that you were coming. Where did you pick that up? Ashore, on port leave, was it?" His gaiety seemed false.

I forbore to say aught about Usher, while, before my eyes, Yanto visibly slumped, his face grey and haggard.

"What is it, Mister? Have you had bad news?" I asked.

His face took a defeated look as he debated inwardly whether to tell me. At last he decided and, near to tears, he whispered, "Dillys has gone." His face seemed deathly pale.

Bit by bit, it came out. His new wife could not face life with a one-legged failure, who had been offered only a cook's berth, or a place at Greenwich Hospital. She had decamped leaving no word of her whereabouts. He stumbled out, saying "That sack is for you, cully."

Bosun's mate Bowlin came next.

"Black Dick has shifted his flag and is at sea in *Defence*," says he, "and the *Queen Charlotte* is goin' on the gridiron at high water tomorrow, matey"

The ship was to be set against the wall, to sit upon a stout structure below as the tide fell, he expounded.

"So as to get at her bottom – the copper 'as been split asunder, and sea water is getting in. The damn'd rats are flooded out an' runnin' everywhere – goddam shambles in the cargo hold. The pusser's goin' mad. Now's yer chance, mate. Doll has spoken for a seat on the carrier's waggon to Dorchester, but it 'ull call in Broadwell tomorrow, and back in two days, so crowd on all yer sail – I've secured an 'ospital pass for 'ee. The carrier goes from the south dockyard gate at two bells o' the forenoon."

Stunned almost speechless, I hardly noticed his second gift of a letter addressed to me at the George until I had stowed a small seabag, thinking all the while of gifts for my grandmother and Eleanour.

Supper for the 'walking mess' was early in the first dog, and at its conclusion, thinking of Yanto's misfortune, I came upon the letter and took it back to the silent mess hall to read privately.

It was from Jenny in a fine slanting hand and clear as a crystal.

'To my dear Prince,

'I bow myself to you, heart of my delight. I cannot set myself free of the passion that has burst forth atween us. Know you that I shall kneel before you in my heart, forever and have sworn thus before my Chief. A woman of the Romanies takes many men in the wild abandon of her nature, but there is only one of whom this oath can be taken. That one is you, gorgio. There is no other.

'Your gift to me was to set me free from whoring, through giving me your first love. You know that to consort with harlots in your country brings ruin to a man, I cannot abet it – only flee from your side in true love.

'Usher was naught – he has escaped our searchers thus far. His true name is Malfort. The one-eyed man you left in France is no Devon fisherman but is called Rabouillet, and he is Malfort's master. Both have broken their bond, by swearing vengeance against one who has been taken into our protection and, since they are without honour, their names may be disclosed. Beware of them, lover.

'Fare well O, Prince. Sadness is upon me at this pass. Having renounced the trade of the harlot I will take none but light Romany sweethearts – they are not lovers. I go now with my tribe to the far Karakorams of our ancestors. As we wander the earth, you will win fame upon the seas, stout sailor, but you will find love again upon the land. Grieve not, my lover.

'Jenny – Your slave for ever.'

I confess that this missive unmanned me completely, and the empty mess hall must have rung with my weeping at the thought I should never see her again. But her beautiful form and her laughter come to me sometimes in the lonely watches of the night, when the sea is her only background and the wind sings soft in the rigging.

That there are many sailors affected likewise, in such times of war, I doubt not. I have come upon them, silently crying, and no battle to account for their grief.

Some days passed before I saw that the names of Malfort and Rabouillet ought to be disclosed to Sir Josiah.

The flagship being grounded, eased the way for an absence, even for one in hospital. The more so since Ned informed me that I was to be rated acting mate and mess-changed, on my return on board.

The carrier set me down without mishap at Broadwell. I looked round for the familiar scenes, but there was naught but rain-swept fields and the grey shadows of trees, bent to the wind.

I hastened into the old familiar Benbow, where the new landlady directed me to Miss Corbett's, saying she was certain I should find her at home. I declined a glass with her, saying I should return before evening, and spoke for a bedroom. A civil curtsey saw me through the door.

I had dreaded the encounter with Miss Eleanour, but when it came, was unprepared for its nature. Gone were the youthful gestures of the schoolroom and she seemed so careworn beyond her years, that I shelved my intended course of confessing an attachment elsewhere.

Eleanour flung her arms about me, bringing confusion as to whether she intended affection or grief, for she burst into tears, causing me to return her embraces out of respect for her obvious distress.

Her form was slender beneath her voluminous nursing garb. "Ah, Andrew," she sobbed. " 'Tis a sad way to greet you thus. I await the coming of Doctor James, to attend your grandmama for I fear the end is near, poor thing.

The good doctor came in accompanied by gusts of rain, and, watch in hand, bustled out again – to attend a birth, having cast a confirming eye over the departure of my poor grandmother. Grandma's face was clouded with the shades of death and her eyes flicked about so helplessly that I near burst forth in a spasm of sobbing. I gulped and swallowed my despair.

She had known poor health for long years, but her claw-like hands grasped my own and I bent to kiss her for one more time. I knelt at her side and at last felt her fingers relax, and slip from my grasp. I thought she had recognised me, for she pressed my hand and murmured, before the light went out of her eyes, and she turned to face whatever fate was in store for her.

Once more my face was awash with tears, and Eleanour was embracing me. It was a struggle to rise from my knees and face the question of the farms' future, and I was ashamed of earthly matters.

My first concern however, was for the interment of grandmother, for whom I was relieved to find there was a place in the churchyard, and in the rain we visited the old lady's last resting place. It was to be with my grandfather under a small blackthorn tree. My mother was expected to attend. Indeed, she was thought to be on her way, having been warned by Eleanour some days before for, I gathered, they had been in correspondence. I was mightily relieved by this, and gave thanks to my benefactress.

On the morrow, I told her, I should have to take a seat on the carrier's waggon back to Portsmouth, where the flagship was to be refloated. But Eleanour, a stranger to the calls of war, was beset with indignant weeping, and flounced from the churchyard under her umbrella.

I protested that the tidings of grandmother's state of health had taken me by surprise, but it would have been of little help in prolonging my stay. I had taken a room at the Benbow and should be vastly obliged to have her company for the evening meal. Before supper I hoped to see the agent for Lord Seckberg. Again I flushed red for my preoccupations.

At that Eleanour stopped in her tracks and, furling her umbrella, turned to face me. "I fear it will not be possible tonight, the agent is away attending the Lord at the races, near Bath," she snapped.

"In that case, I shall try my fortune with Sir John Blunder, and pray that you will be able to afford me the heartfelt pleasure of your company at supper."

When we sat down to supper in the Benbow's dining room, Eleanour was more her old self, dressed not in the height of a London ladies' fashion, but prettily gowned for all that, and she seemed surprised at my rig too. Before I left Portsmouth Doll had provided me with a jacket 'befitting a gentleman about to take his post on the quarterdeck', as the tailor had assured her.

"Andrew Miller, am I to understand you have received promotion? I do believe all those buttons betoken something other than a seaman. Pray tell me, you do not sail under false colours, sir." She seemed vastly amused now.

I settled her misgivings, though from her smiles I was satisfied that she toyed with me. Instead I gave her an account of my visit to Sir John's manor house. The squire was pleased to receive me, and I saw that his opinion had changed with regard to my mother.

He was also perceptive enough to see from my new coat that I had been given a step up to mate, or rather apprenticeship in that rating, trusting it to keep Lord Seckberg in check.

He knew more than I suspected about the enclosure of the farms, for he held a seat on the County enquiry into land ownership. He reassured me that that he would look into the case, and I signed a letter to the attorney who had earlier informed me of my inheritance, to empower his acting on my behalf.

With a puffing and blowing, Sir John said, "He ain't afraid of that German bugger's influence, lad – no more ain't I – Seckberg, I mean. If it will help your cause, you might change your name to Blunder, hey? Then they'll all comprehend they have a Blunder to deal with, lad."

I gave Eleanour the gist of this talk, and her demeanour became more relieved. However she bridled a little, I thought, when the Benbow's landlady appeared to enquire if we received satisfactory attention, and offering a bottle of fine wine.

In due course, I learned that this creature had been selected by my mother for her capable airs and graces, though not one of the village could recall hearing tell of her before. There being no other applicant, mother's approaching wedding had driven away any doubts. Yet she was a veritable dark horse.

We saw she intended to join us at the table and I noted signs of disapproval flit across Eleanour's face. She fell silent on discussing Sir John and Lord Seckberg before the landlady.

Instead, with the arrival of the wine, she introduced the

landlady as Mistress Jamieson, adding the information that she was lately in Lord Seckberg's employ. This was accompanied by a smart kick to my ankle, below the flowing drapes of the table.

I pondered this warning, but seeing nothing further of significance, resolved to drop the subject, and to my surprise, I became embroiled in Mistress Jamieson's flood of enquiry, compliment and smiling tattle. It was a shock to perceive looks of distaste crossing Eleanour's face and I assumed her foot had been employed under the table. She had noticed that the landlady had changed her dress and now wore a display of jewellery at her throat which fell to a sumptuous bosom. Below sparkling eyes her cheeks seemed brighter than nature intended.

The landlady pressed my wrist, and gushed that I must be Mister Miller, the son of a former landlady. Did I still own two farms, she wondered? Of course I recognised that rural village life bred gossip and she had made it her business to be informed.

Eleanour, who expected me to walk with her to her home, recalled me to this duty, and asked for her cloak, to Mistress Jamieson's obvious discomfiture. But she rose to the occasion, saying brightly, that her groom would drive her through the nasty puddles, in the covered pony trap. It would save Mister Miller the walk back too.

Eleanour was equal to this sally.

"Such a kind thought, Mrs Jamieson; it does you credit which I shall not forget, I am sure, but fear it may be the last time convenient for Andrew" – she paused to emphasise her familiar use of my name – "to inspect his late grandmother's belongings. He takes ship tomorrow, alas – is that not so?"

She turned to me, displaying some echoes of the old

mischief of her schoolroom days, and I could not but confirm her coup, which Eleanour followed with a display of surprise.

"Oh, Mrs Jamieson, perhaps you were not aware that we have had so sad a bereavement this morning."

The landlady lowered her head in understanding, but I detected a look of triumph, perhaps in the thought that I must return afterwards to her clutches.

The feeling of being a shuttlecock between the two embattled ladies, welled up in me so that I could hardly suppress my laughter.

CHAPTER 12

The flagship was engaged in victualling and replacing her spoiled stores and my presence was dispensed with, though my arm was regaining its power under a regime of exercise that the surgeons imposed, and the master-at-arms supervised with sabre drill and a malicious grin.

I learned that there was a berth reserved for me in the gun room and was set to correct the charts that Yanto had presented to me at the hospital, but of my disabled friend I saw nothing, for he was discharged 'to shore' like a ship passed in the night.

At the George, Doll gave me a tearful embrace, but I saw Rosie entangled with a red marine, and she avoided my eye – to my great satisfaction.

I gave Doll a letter from Eleanour, which she scanned and informed me that the lady thanked her for services to me, and proposed to visit Portsmouth as soon as the funeral rites were done. She supposed that, by then, I should be sailing the seas.

As Doll remarked, Pompey would doubtless be a shock and eye-opener to this parson's widow, and she wondered what had possessed her to resume her maiden name.

"You have the gals a-flocking after you, my lad," she pronounced as if there was no disputing what was a fact, established to her satisfaction and she triumphantly produced her evidence in a strong Irish brogue.

"Yer ma has written from Devon about some sewing I did for her, you know," she commenced with her fine talent for switching the subject, especially to gossip. She gripped my arm in a fine state of animation and I sensed another of Doll's gale-force tirades blowing up and sought to forestall it.

"And how did you find my mother, when she visited the George?" I asked hastily.

"Ah the darling lady! Perhaps she was a wee touch delicate o' the marnings, y'know. 'Twas naught to spake of, a burden we women have to shoulder, 'tis naught."

She clapped my shoulder. "Sure she was fit as a flea from the O'Grady's bog, whenever I gave her my Oirish receipt for ut. 'Twas the baby y'know!"

Puzzled, I studied Doll curiously.

"I thought young William would have been running about by now. Why, I brought a wooden hoop for him to give chase to."

Doll eyed me in return and burst forth in torrent of nervous chatter. "Ah me dear boy, I can see you know nothing at all. Yer ma is with child again – that major is mighty potent, I'd say. I'm thinking maybe she might give you a wee girl – a sister for you and William."

She paused and called for "a shot o' that best brandy for the master's mate and meself."

We drank heartily to safe arrival of a new sister – or a brother. But in her usual fashion, she recalled her previous subject of complaint – Mrs Meg Fellowes.

"That Meg woman, the forward wench, wants to see you, and all. Oh, a smart lass, Oi'll grant you, but too old, for all the saints. Sure an' she fancies herself, wouldn't even spake to Ned at all."

Thumping the table she glared at my sudden interest.

"Divil, the lad!"

I resolved to inform Lt Bashem and Sir Josiah about Meg. The former walked with me to the master's cabin, a palace when compared with his own canvas abode. Mr Shaw, the master, was senior in position, but, as a warrant officer, would never surpass the lieutenants in command. It was more plain between the master and his mates, and he jumped up and seized my hand.

"Just the man, just the man, you're wanted in the dockyard, Miller – on board the *Black Joke*. That Probyn man has need of your undoubted talents for a special task. It seems the ship is to be commissioned again. I shall not guess her task, but it is not beyond Ushant to my mind, so don't look for blackstrap. I haven't stowed her for the tropics either." He grinned evilly, and I guessed he was making reference to his duty to authorise stores.

"But you'll not want for black paint, my boy, nor dark sail dressing." He roared with laughter at his own humour, then looked serious, saying. "I wish you luck, lad."

As we left the cabin, Jemmy Bashem resolved my puzzlement at once.

"The *Black Joke* sails on the morning tide, Miller, and I'm to ask you if you're fit to join us – and willing, for you've had rough weather of it lately. It is another raid on L'Aberwrac'h, and I asked the flag captain for you, but he was concerned for your health."

I do not know what possessed me but my eagerness was plain to see, causing Bashem to hold up his hand and tell me that the *Black Joke* would be under the command of the Honourable Rupert de Bach. From this I deduced that the captain had succumbed to some wealthy nobleman's pressure to improve his protégé's experience by a command at sea. *Black Joke* was a tender to the Flag.

"Sir, I wish to volunteer," I said simply, not even asking what my role would be in this venture.

"You ship as navigator, Andrew", he replied. "Sir Josiah Probyn wishes that urgent intelligence be gathered, and I will take command of the landing party. Marines on horseback!" he cackled like a schoolboy.

The ship's company mustered on deck, facing the two lieutenants, when Jemmy stepped to the binnacle.

"Lieutenant de Bach has command, and he has asked me to detail the plan of this little banyan party. Due to the fogs of the past weeks, our inshore frigates haven't a notion of the state of the Monsoors in Brest. Perchance they are not at home, lads, and have stepped out for a banyan of their own. There were thirty of the line, but at least two have been sighted off Spanish Finisterra, steering westward, and several more from Toulon have passed Gibraltar into the Atlantic.

"Their fishermen have disappeared off the seas too – maybe detained in port. What is happening, do you suppose? We are to act as the eyes of his honour, Black Dick, and must get some news from Brest."

Jemmy struggled to contain his laughter as he spoke next. "We know there are ample hosses in L'Aberwrac'h and we are charged to become horse thieves, to mount a reconnaissance on Brest, with twelve 'Jollies', disguised as ploughmen." He grinned at me. "If you'd be so kind to land us, captain." He turned, touching his hat to Rupert.

"This raid is different from the last. Instead of landing from ship's boats your captain intends to take the *Black Joke* in with the aid of Mister Miller, acting mate, who has been there before. We shall go in by the western entrance and hold the port till the 'Jolly' cavalry returns, and, for God's sake, hack their bloody guillotine down, it gives me the shakes – aye, without the aid of Jamaica rum."

"My lads!" he chaffed them, "you'll be dismayed to know there ain't any forts or gun batteries to entertain us – my apologies – but Parker has a little packet aft under that canvas, a 'long nine', in case they bring up some gallopers to harass our departure on the tide."

On board the flagship Jemmy was well liked as one who knew the problems of the lower deck men, and bantered with them in their own language. Besides, he knew the ground ahead and plainly controlled the green Rupert.

Jack Parker, gunner's mate, was new, having been drafted on board barely a week before. He was a veritable dab with guns, it was said. But he had an arrogant manner and a short fused temper. They would see.

All Rupert said was, "I shall splice the main brace before dinner – good luck, you men." It was said in a self-conscious manner, but it went a long way after we had turned to with black paint for the side and dark dye for the sails – not unusual for a fishing vessel.

Off St Catherine's Point on the Isle of Wight, I turned in my hammock, reeling from the labour of that day, but not despondent. Rather I was keyed up by the prospect of action. The plan to approach Brest from inland, on horses, seemed a good one with people fluent in French, such as Bashem, but was it tempting fate to keep a cutter long in a French harbour?

I fell asleep to the familiar movement of the billows below our keel, thinking that I had not worried all day about the farms or my duties to the ladies to whom I was beholden.

Next day, Bashem, Mr de Bach and I pored over the charts to point out the approaches to the port, our target.

"The northern passage will not serve in these light winds, although the tide will favour us in the western entrance, unless the wind hauls round easterly. There's shoal ground here." His finger stubbed the chart. "Of course I leave the rounding up to the quay in your hands,

Rupert, but beg to recommend dropping your hook about here, then snubbing her round and veering your cable till we reach the quay." He ably acted the part of a senior man giving advice only.

"Miller knows the quayside well, do you not, Miller? Haw haw! Now I must see to the landing party."

By next evening the cutter had felt its way through fog to the westerly entrance, the breeze scarcely stirring the billows of mist. Only with the flooding tide would we have headway in this calm. At last we were able to weigh and move slowly between the shoals and rocks.

Round the vessel the silent lookouts peered into the dripping murk, and in the eye of the ship a hand stood to for the order to let go the anchor again.

As the protégé of the flagship's sailing master, I stood at the tiller with the *Black Joke*'s quartermaster, and, from scribbles in my notebook, was able to warn him of the course to the next.

"I see you're ready with the brails and halliards, captain," Bashem whispered and the skipper relaxed his hold on the binnacle somewhat.

All round the deck men waited at instant readiness, the only noise being the tide gurgling round the dripping rocks and under the ship's stem. Parker, the gunner's mate, strained on the run out tackles of his new gun, and felt to make sure the rams were ready to hand. He coughed loudly in the foggy air, causing the captain to jump and spin round.

"You bloody fool," he snapped. "Stow your gob, can you not?" He trailed off, knowing that he had made more noise than a dozen men coughing.

"Rock right ahead." I whispered.

"Good man, leave it to starboard, helmsman." Rupert was redeeming himself.

The tidal stream seemed to have gathered strength. Glancing overhead, I thought the mist was blowing away and prayed that it was not.

"Four or five cables to go, captain, I reckon."

Time seemed to stand still as we drifted slowly on. Steerage way was difficult to hold. I sent another hand forward to help with the anchor.

The captain took the hint. "Stand by anchor." His voice still had the quality of a bellowing bull in our enclosed world of near-silence. Suddenly a shaft of dawn's sun, almost horizontal, pierced our white canopy and a little port was revealed before us as the shreds of mist thinned.

"My God," breathed Bashem explosively, "French corvettes! Stand by larboard broadside. Your pardon, captain, the honour is yours."

Two French vessels, each larger than *Black Joke*, were made fast at the quay. These were *Cotillion* and *Quadrille*. Strangely, the nearest, *Cotillion*, had all her ports open but no guns appeared. On the quayside a huge mound of timber stood, blocking the view beyond the corvettes. There was no movement in either ship.

Rupert gaped and his tongue rattled in his throat. "Stand by larboard," he repeated lamely.

"May I suggest snub round the anchor, captain," came Bashem's voice, rising to a strangled bellow. "Shoals ahead, man." He stood straight before the binnacle, arm fully raised, then slashed it down in the universal signal to let go the anchor. "Sheets and halliards," he shouted and our mainsail came down.

The cable shirred through the fairlead, until the anchor bit and held in the seabed. The cutter slowed and began a half circle round the anchor, propelled by the tidal stream.

Grasping the position, Rupert ordered the cable to be

veered, and we travelled stern first towards the corvettes.

At this point Rupert realised he must attend to the guns. "Fire as you bear," he screeched and the gun captains touched off their vents. Parker's shot hit the stone quay, raising a shower of stone chips, while another ball bounded into the great pile of timber, causing it to collapse and a thin spiral of smoke to arise.

"Hold on to your cable," I yelled. And our progress was halted. We were close, almost abreast of the first corvette.

I leapt to the forecastle of the corvette *Cotillion* whence I could sight the ground hidden behind the timber. The corvette's crews were gathered round the inn among a swarm of revelling villagers, and I saw that the guillotine still stood. A lone French seaman was running towards them, from the quay, shouting and waving, and I knew that he, at least, had discovered our arrival.

"Go for her masts," bawled Rupert, pointing, and the gun captains took their quoins to elevate the muzzles. The first concerted broadsides brought down some spars, but, as the guns recoiled on their breechings, a foul black smoke enveloped them, and they saw no more, scrambling back to their positions in a frenzy of well-remembered drill that is the hallmark of British tars.

The hubbub at the inn ceased at our broadside, and folk ran hither and thither. At the blare of a trumpet, some turned and ran the other way, thinking it was the 'Retreat.' However the gun smoke soon told them otherwise, and a disorderly advance on the quay developed.

"Sir," I confronted the captain. "The Frogs are all about a mile away. They know something is amiss from the noise of our guns, but cannot see us – but a warning is on the way. Their guns have been landed t'other side of the woodpile, and they will have to come at us from there. I recommend we have grapeshot ready to meet them."

I was shouldered aside roughly by Bashem. "Impossible to catch those horses under the noses of the Frogs. So I will make an attempt on the other corvette with marines."

"Sergeant," he shouted, "tell them to remove those bloody spurs, they'll start a fire with all this loose powder about." Parker glared, nettled at the alleged spillage.

"All hands take up the anchor cable," continued Bashem, "and let us see your beef in pulling the barky back agin flood tide – you agree, captain?"

Nervously Rupert inclined his head in assent.

The hauling party was joined by all the seamen that could be spared, the cook and his mate and the gunner's party among them. It was 'stamp and go' all up the decks, until at last the *Black Joke* began to move. It was near the top of the tide and soon there would be a stand, then the stream would start to ebb in the other direction.

At once I obtained the captain's attention again. "Sir I believe the Frenchmen are rigging the first corvette as a fire ship. There are stacks of barrels on the quay that smell of tar, I think, and below decks there are piles of wood, smelling the same."

Rupert came to life at that. The presence of the corvettes in daylight, followed by the new revelations, made our escape highly unlikely, for the enemy could command us with their guns on shore. The situation kept changing, but I assumed a ride to Brest on horseback was cancelled.

"We could burn them, sir," I suggested.

"An excellent notion, Mr Miller, and what, pray, for corvette number two?"

"I believe Mr Bashem wishes to board her, before the

Frenchmen return. After that we could send down fireboats from here on floating lines, and set them alight with heated grapeshot or fuses, if it can be done before the ebb."

The captain pursed his lips and then beamed. "By George, yes! Serve the Frogs at their own scurvy game hey?"

He repeated the notion to Bashem, who was immersed in his landing party's fortunes. "Axes here, pass them into the boat – away boarders, starboard."

At that moment the first French gun opened fire. They had re-sited it well ahead of the *Cotillion* and dug it in to prevent the recoil, and at such a range it smashed through our bulwarks removing some vital standing rigging. A backstay sagged precariously.

"Cable party, bring to the capstan," I called and, as the turns were taken, a second ball whistled over our deck, smashing through our starboard bulwarks to plunge harmlessly into the harbour over the heads of the landing party's boat.

The capstan was hauling *Black Joke* through the water slowly, but continuously spoiling the aim of the two shore guns, when Rupert called out, "Helm over hard, slack on the capstan." The ship veered away from the quayside so that our stern swung in toward the ragged beach, giving a slant view of the French guns.

"Parker," roared the captain, "take out that battery to larboard."

After some sighting shots, Parker scored a hit on the nearest of the French guns, exploding their box of gun charges, and spreading flying debris over the second gun, to wild cheers from *Black Joke*'s crew, which cut off abruptly when a French ball soared over and upset the long nine, trapping Parker underneath.

In Bashem's boat, a musket ball tore across the forearm of the second stroke, causing him to lose his oar and collapse, writhing on his thwart. Jemmy seized a spare oar and took his place.

"Now lads, I'm setting the stroke, so put your idle backs into it. We have to get into the other corvette's lee smartly, and board her."

The oarsmen needed no urging, for the musket fire was becoming warmer as the Frenchmen advanced, causing sharp splinters of wood to fly everywhere.

In the bows, the marine at the boat's gun shouted, "Over there sir, they are under the trees – muskets only."

Three marines scrambled forward, to stand in the foresheets behind the gunner, and, as heads appeared above the bank, fired a volley, which cleared the skyline.

The French crewmen rallied and came streaming over the top, chanting in unison, when the boat's gun fired its round of grapeshot and sent them reeling back. By this time the jollyboat reached the cover of the corvette, and the screaming marines scrambled on board the flush-decked vessel, to lay about themselves with their axes.

First the ropes to the quay were attacked, while the bare-footed Jemmy stove in the gunner's kegs with an axe swathed in canvas to avoid sparks. He poured the powder in trails about the magazine. The ship's bow was in midstream now, carried there by the last of the flood before any of the French crew came to the water's edge. There was no time for setting her alight now and the jolly boat alongside was fast filling with departing boarders, more than ready to be gone. Jemmy was last to drop into the boat, having first hacked off the ship's stern ropes.

"Hold on to that painter," shouted Jemmy to one of the marines. "We'll ride under the *Quadrille*'s lee as long as maybe. Those damned Frogs will wonder where we've gone."

The destination of the unmanned *Quadrille* was an outcrop of vicious tree-fringed rocks opposite the port, but before she was stranded, the jolly boat was rowed clear, and pulling for the *Black Joke*.

"Gunner's mate 'ave copped one," muttered a sweating hand at the foremost thwart. "Poor sod won't come nosing round no more – Nosey Parker!" The body of the gunner's mate still lay huddled on the deck above them.

"Stow it, Evans. Save your breath for that damned oar. It'll do more good for you than your old whore in Pompey. I'll be bound."

The hands grinned and, gritting their teeth, bent their backs to drive the boat across the exposed stretch of water. Only a few musket balls kicked up jets of water astern of them and they came at last under the lee of the *Black Joke*.

Bashem swung on board the cutter, hasting to the captain's side with his arm outstretched, pointing over the quay. "They have an officer there, and draw more guns to waylay us when the ebb starts, d'ye not see!"

Rupert indicated the helm hard over to steer off the shore.

"It is done – I am steering away from the quay, Jemmy. But we will not profit until there is some strength in the ebb tide to get us moving. I have directed Miller to move the starboard guns across the ship to replace the two upset by Monsieur Frog. Our broadside will be complete that side, but how I yearn for the long nine."

Rupert raised a hand and I, in turn, signalled the battery to open fire. At the mercy of the tide we were not in a perfect position for great success, but nor was the enemy for we were both partly hidden by scrub and saplings.

Nevertheless our larboard guns laid down a quite creditable rate of fire. The Frenchmen's guns put forth a shower of balls, more slowly than ours but coming closer at each volley. I saw they had officers among the trees, directing fire and I was able to interfere by aiming our musketry at them and their runners. It became a game of measure and counter-measure.

A message from the aft came to me, and I rushed there in time to find that Parker had called out. I knelt over the deathly pale man to find his free arm moving. He held out a black scarf, saying, "Bear a hand, mate, and pass a seizing on this."

Binding the arm tight, I pulled him out with the aid of some marines, who lifted and righted the gun. Before he lost his senses again, Parker breathed, "She's a fine gun, Miller – will reach that damn barky from here." They carried him below.

The sun was still high in the sky but cloud was building up from the North, bringing stinging bouts of rain and low cloud, which drifted amongst the streaming trees. I discovered the captain's talent lay chiefly in gunnery, for he came aft in the lowering visibility and took charge of the loading and training of the restored long-nine.

His 'Now, where's our target, Miller?' was satisfied when I pointed to a bright glow in the deepening mist. "It is the woodpile alongside *Cotillion*, sir". Rupert sighted along the barrel and, warning his crew, fired the gun.

Two more shots followed and at the third came a great eruption, with blasts at intervals, caused, we thought, by barrels hidden amongst the fuel for a fire ship. Whether they were from within the *Cotillion*'s hold or the cargo heaped alongside the ship, we could not tell but it certainly restored Rupert's standing with the crew.

The harrowing task of navigating the return passage exhausted all our company, for we did not emerge from the winding passage until late in the first watch. Wisely the captain chose to anchor till the end of the middle, with a liberal ration of rum in our bellies.

On doing rounds of the ship, I found we had suffered a heavy butcher's bill in total, mostly caused by flying splinters and crushed limbs. Next day there were three to bury at sea, sewn into their hammocks. Two seamen and one marine went overboard and once more I saw Jemmy Bashem sunk in a sense of failure. As we all were.

There was much splicing and rigging to carry out before we could raise even a jury rig on our mast, and we fretted all the daylight hours, keeping a heavy armed guard, for fear of the enemy discovering our whereabouts.

During this breathless interlude, Jemmy and I were intrigued to see Rupert delight in his command. Luckily, our boats were little damaged and our captain was first to order fishing expeditions for all the men to eat well.

Bashem seemed keen to stand the night watches, and it was a shock to discover a newcomer in the cutter on the second morning. On my taking the day watch, a garrulous lookout took pains to inform me of Jemmy's habit of showing lanterns at night but he was disappointed of me in the way of scuttlebutt for I was not in the secret.

It was later in the forenoon that I encountered a familiar face, that of Sir Josiah Probyn. His disarming grin and a silent handshake did not hide his battered countenance, and he went below without a word of explanation. I knew enough of him to avoid questions – though I was mighty curious.

After three days had passed, days of worsening weather, we were able to depart for Portsmouth. We were at sea

BATTLE OFF PRAWLE POINT

mid-Channel when Sir Josiah, known only to the crew as 'mister', motioned me to the wardroom. It was a small compartment, unoccupied at that moment by anyone else, even the mess servant.

Probyn invited me to take a chair whilst he poured two glasses of what I thought was Burgundy wine.

He had become assured of my discretion in dealing with what he cheerfully called 'Whitehall matters'. He lifted his glass to my advancement and beamed. "Genuinely delighted, old friend", he said and we settled to talk of random subjects, mainly of interest to sailors, for he knew us and our interests as closely as if he were one himself.

"Sad to say, Petty Officer Bowlin could not be on this escapade, or banyan, as you call it, hey?"

He grinned widely, and reached for the wine again, 'restoring our glasses', as he termed it. I must have shown signs of worry, for he became hearty at once.

"Never you fret about keeping your watch, my lad. Captain Rupert is taking the deck himself tonight. It should be his last chance, providing we make the Needles channel on time – his last chance I feel because he looks to go as number one of a frigate. Fast work, I fancy!"

"De Bach is fortunate, though," mused Probyn aloud, "and so am I, sir. Especially am I grateful to be waited upon by the good ship *Black Joke*, but our captain is lucky to escape with his ship – and with one corvette blown up and another stranded, sinking, hey?" He did not mention the first hand confirmation that the French were preparing fire ships. We both lapsed into silence and weighed in our minds the fortunes of war.

"Do I guess that you know his successor here, sir", I ventured at last.

"Aye, and so do you, sir," he twinkled.

I just looked mystified, being amused by his coyness. I could not attribute it to the wine for Probyn was too much in command of himself at all times.

"It is good news to most of the hands here – those who knew him, when he had hopes of commanding the Joke, himself", he said.

"Ah sir, then you do mean Mr Hempe, I collect. An excellent choice, sir," I smirked playing him at his game.

"My good fellow, I would say you have me to rights. Well done, Miller. Hempe, poor fellow, was deprived before, due to the *Black Joke*'s peculiar fitness for ferreting round the Breton coast. I thought it right for him to have her, for he is a blunt man, though not fitted for 'Whitehall matters' this time. It is a modest enough reward, eh?"

Having seen Mr Hempe's anguish, I could not but agree, and felt like a Sultan at being informed of a change.

Probyn edged closer, after re-filling his glass once again. I saw marks on his face of healed-up injuries, recently inflicted, and felt incensed but I made no comment.

"This is for your ears, my lad, but you may certainly confide in Bowlin, if you wish – I ran foul of Mr 'U' ashore and learned that your friend Miss Forward and her father were both held prisoner by him and his chief, whom you know of."

This talented man could not know that this 'Miss' had sworn to be true to me – and that my feelings were as deep toward her. I think he intended to stop at this point.

Now he saw my stricken face. His attitude was become changed abruptly, and his jocular manner vanished as he stared intently at me. I was to learn something too of the code of conduct under which our spies laboured – since he was no less than that.

Probyn set down his glass in the rack, for the cutter was

rolling now as dark seas crashed against her sides. Had he decided to give me more news of Jenny?

"At present I cannot say where your lover is, because this information came from an agent of mine, a trusted fellow and colleague. He is not given to inaccuracies I assure you, and had no reason to think that such news was of concern to us. He had picked up their trail near Fecamp.

"The Romney Marsh men do much of their trade there, and he knew of other Romanies who had landed from England of late, horses, wheeled carts and all.

"Now this agent is working for us on a highly dangerous mission. We cannot risk such a valuable servant of Admiralty. We cannot disclose his identity unless you have positive leave to go to France and seek your friends, which I have reason to judge is becoming less and less likely. I cannot say more.

"Now sir, I counsel you to think it over. Your friends are not in immediate danger, I suspect. 'U' wants chiefly to mend his relations with the lady, but Rabouillet will do anything to advance the odious Minister of Marine's plans and scupper Lord Howe's."

Probyn stood. "I must go to my hammock now – beastly canvas contraption – but you may seek me out. Bowlin knows how. Good night and good luck to you."

I went on deck to think. My mind was in a spin but, to my annoyance, I was not to have the solitude I craved.

The lookout was reporting to Rupert, "Land fine on the starboard bow, sir. Shore lights on the bearing."

It was the Needles rocks, and there was satisfaction in the seaman's voice for a home-coming. There was no leisure for my thoughts – nor for Rupert's on his last night in command.

CHAPTER 13

The life in Lord Howe's flagship to which I was returned was to be far different from that of a gun deck mess which I once had. Master's mates were accommodated in the gunroom on the orlop deck. It was right aft on the lowest deck and never saw the light o' day, lit as it was by candle lanterns and bounded by sheets of canvas.

The distance kept by my former messmates of the gun deck spelt a rather less boisterous company for me but, while it was a relief to be done with the constant blasphemous language, I had relished the grotesque, often accidental, humour employed by Jack Tar.

Now a sea change was come upon me. It is true that I still saw much of the seaman complement, having the duty to work with them, when not consorting with the officers in their duties. But they doubtless noted my serious, unsmiling look on return from L'Aberwrac'h. With Sir Josiah's warnings in mind, I had to guard my tongue constantly. On passing an old messmate, I often imagined a humorous jibe was about to be thrown at me, only to see it stifled, a greeting left unsaid.

Most did not know what to do about this 'jumped-up' chancer, who had turned out to be a land owner and an unknown quantity out of the ship. Perhaps they counted him a viper they had nursed in their bosoms.

However, it is not unusual for 'servants' to be promoted midshipman or mate and other advancements were common enough, and I tried to ignore it.

We were expected to dress 'as befits an officer', at least on the quarterdeck, and from some time past it had become normal for mates to face an oral examination in practical seamanship, as for midshipmen. It might lead to commissioning as a 'sea officer' in the rank of lieutenant.

The gunroom often saw the baiting of some mates and midshipmen, but the goal of becoming a lieutenant was deemed of paramount importance in a naval career, for we knew that all captains and admirals had come up the ladder the same way. Most of us strove therefore.

Many shore tailors had similar ideas of what was befitting an officer and I found that other mates in the gunroom wore what amounted to an unofficial uniform. Their choice was a plain blue coat with plenty of shining buttons atop white breeches or trousers, with an absence of gold lace, But, after all, I was sure that Doll would not be palmed off with anything less than correct.

In the gunroom I encountered a Mr Hector Collins. A mate of mature age who ruled us as 'lord and master', for, being close to five and thirty years, it was alleged, he might assert the right of seniority over us, if not over the midshipmen. Of course everything to do with the quarterdeck was ruled by seniority, jealously guarded.

Collins was a whimsical fellow with a head of bright auburn curls, who was prone to address us with hysterical laughter. He seldom appeared above deck level, they said or assayed anything that smacked of manual labour, especially if it involved oil or tar. He was a creature of the quarter deck, confining his attentions to perfecting our charts and tables. It was said he was a born draughtsman and earned the name of 'Mr Drafty.'

Annually Mr Collins had to endure the chagrin of appearing before a board of captains for a lieutenant's place, an encounter that led invariably to failure, and the two other mates assured me that he laughed for days.

Mr Collins' seniority, of course, advanced with his age

and there was speculation that he might be posted in command of a stationary boom vessel, except that his gleaming white breeches were markedly unsuitable for that station, and would surely become soiled. It was said there was a powerful 'interest' at the back of him, which would be affronted by such a lowly appointment.

Being morose and surly, I am sure the gunroom did not find my company at all congenial. The fate of Jenny and her father hung over me to the exclusion of much else and I was obsessed with frustration and despair. The only person I could consult with was Ned, for I was uncertain how much could be disclosed to anyone else, even Jemmy Bashem.

Ned was out of the ship, I was told. He was the passport to Sir Josiah, but I recalled that the chief spy seemed doubtful of making a sidetrack to the Fecamp area of Normandy or back to Brest.

It was possible that the flag captain might lend a sympathetic ear, but he had already seemed to be glad to distance himself from the world of secret agents and less inclined therefore to interfere with matters outside the *Queen Charlotte*.

I cudgelled my brain to light upon anyone who might have sufficient knowledge at least to locate my lover of such brief standing. Names like Meg, the partner of the late Mr Fellowes, seemed possible, or Shimey or the officer of the law who had commandeered our boat to chase Usher across to Gosport. To clap eyes on and meet with any one of them might still not remove the problem.

Even if a fruitful possibility turned up in my head, it was likely that Mr Shaw, the master, would be extremely averse to furnishing leave for another absence from duty.

He seemed obsessed with advancing my navigational

skills – there were new improvements arising all the time to be mastered and installed, such as the Harrison timepiece. I have to confess, for example, that I was woefully lacking in celestial navigation. I had no schooling in the noonday sighting of the sun and less for the stars, yet even young midshipmen had undergone it. All my hours outside those spent on watch on the quarterdeck, dull and uneventful routines as they might be, went in assisting Mr Collins at his charts.

Eight bells in the morning next day was marked by the presence on the quarterdeck of troops of senior officers in formal rig. It was a sight seldom seen, for the admiral's staff worked in many a burrow. The admiral and part of his staff were to shift to another ship.

The ceremony itself took little time, consisting only of striking Black Dick's flag from the main, to the tune of 'Hearts of Oak', and the withdrawal of the senior officers afterwards was not prolonged by a public gossip, for the wind inclined to bluster and was driving scuds of cold rain before it. The *Queen Charlotte* was become a 'private ship.'

Black Dick had left her the day before, ostensibly to throw a grand reception – a 'rout', as it was described, since it had to be seen to attract a large number of the notables from the county of Hampshire. For this the admiral had the use of the lord lieutenant's residence – a grand country house. The ship's domestic staff were to be in attendance too. Thereafter, the admiral was to hoist his flag in a frigate to inspect the shores of Brittany once more. To my astonishment I heard that Ned Bowlin was to be at the rout too.

Bashem, the fourth lieutenant, was not to attend the rout, having been dispatched to join parties from other ships in a grand press gang. Its object was to recruit or press merchant seamen out of a large convoy, homeward bound from the East Indies. Boats' crews were also supplied by other ships of the Channel fleet, and it was reckoned that Jemmy's role would be subordinate and unremarkable. Before sunset I saw them sail in two cutters of the *Defence*, a 74 of the Van. They were making for the eastern entrance to the Solent with ships' boats under Jemmy in tow. Other ships would act at the Needles Channel for merchantmen choosing that route.

It was obvious that there was still a severe shortage in recruiting but I thought little of it. I would venture ashore in the hope of taking a drink with Doll, and needing to repay the money she'd laid out for my new rig.

The appearance of a mate in the taproom of the George was not sufficient to raise eyebrows, and besides, many of the clients recognised me. Had they not, Doll's wild Irish yell would have apprised them of my identity.

She rushed my unprepared defences and enfolded me in her arms, roaring and weeping like 'a banshee in the bog', as Ned was wont to phrase it.

"Ah there y'are, me darlin'," she informed me, to ironic cheers from the dockyard mateys. "I heard ye had some fellers killed over there, didya?"

I flinched at her loud question, but supposed that the existence of wounded men could not be swept under the carpet, after being ferried to Haslar, nor the fate of those buried at sea denied by their messmates who auctioned the dead mens' kits, as the custom demanded.

Doll muttered, "Ye're right then, ye're right! And my Rose wept all night, so she did. Oi'll have you to know she's done wid that eejit longshoreman all because of you!"

My confidence sagged as my fears were justified. Doll

was about to propose the union of Rosie with myself, at which she'd been hinting for months. She cocked an eye at me and handed me a mug of ale as she nerved herself to apprise me of what was already a certainty and a case of public knowledge, or rather it was sure to be so within the walls of the George.

I quaked – surely not on the strength of one kiss at a celebratory gathering!

"That one's me own favourite, yiz know – the apple o' me eye and she'd lay down and die for ye, don't you know?" she asserted.

I managed to keep a straight face, agreeing that Rosie would make some fellow a handsome wee wife, but I could not recommend a sailor for such a tender blossom – too much sailing off and leaving wives or sweethearts to weep on the pier head, did she not think?

I knew Doll's views on sailors from the way she hectored the unshakeable Ned on the subject.

That was surely the end of the matter, and it was out at last. I resolved to say naught concerning the marines and soldiers that Rosie paraded about the wharves and lanes of Old Portsmouth but drank my ale mug dry in one great gulp.

Turning to face the buxom housekeeper, I could not hide the smile that creased my face, and saw Doll's face similarly inflicted. At that we fell into great gusts of laughter, delighted the subject no longer lay in wait between us. Not once had Doll admitted that Rosie was her daughter.

Now that the air was clear, Doll got down to some serious talking, not omitting interrogations. She demanded a full account of the death of my grandmother and railed against me for not attending the funeral. I formed the opinion that, even after all her time with Ned, she had not grasped the notion that in the Navy the timetable of a ship rules the roost. Even the dullest country fellow knows that 'time and tide waiteth for no man'.

As a hotel housekeeper she recognised that there were social functions for the gentry, but was mystified by Ned's inclusion in Lord Howe's supper, as she called it. I had first been puzzled too, but it occurred to me that it was the doing of Sir Josiah.

Whether she was driven by jealousy of Ned's 'shenanigans' I failed to fathom, but it started her on a rant of frustration that went on and on, not in keeping with her normal jollity.

Doll took another drink – and another. Her sensibilities may have dissolved in laughter on one count, but on the next she was given to a loud halloo about other women. Reaching for the cognac again she would raise her slurred voice, aimed at I knew not what.

"And phwat is this I hear, I pray you, about that Meg woman? She's been 'ere asking after youse, young feller. Why she's more o' that divil Ned's mark, so she is?"

My hopes were thus raised on the instant at discovering in Meg a route, or rather a lead, to Jenny and her father, without posing the question myself.

Doll, however, remained unaware of my brightened eyes, carrying on with her assessment of Meg's character that was distinctly unflattering, and to which I apply an editorial brush, in the interests of propriety. But now it was obvious that Doll was over-assiduous at the bottle.

"Faith, no better than she should be, is that one. You'll know she's a Frog woman, I may suppose?"

She swayed alarmingly. "In Paris they're all whores, you know. The worst of 'em wears ribbons o' scarlet at their necks, representin' the road to perdition under the Jilloteen. I tell yiz, a t'ousand Hail Mary's will niver save that one. I shall not tell yiz how those sluts escape the Jilloteen; across the water; 'twould be the ruin o' ye to hear it, so it would." Her head was nodding and her eyes drooped – a state I never thought to see in Doll.

"You keep clear o' that Meg, I say, she's offal, an' isn't she forever runnin' to the coroner wid her tales, so I'm told. Is ut true, d'ye think?"

"It's of no account, Doll," I whispered. "What could a French biddy know that is of interest to us, or to Ned. I don't even know where she lives, if it is not at Fellowe's farm. I hear that it is for sale."

At this Doll came to life, anxious perhaps to show a greater knowledge of gossip than Ned or me. She spilled scandal to me at once.

"Arrah, she's at that hole, the Golden Cross, servin' in the snug, and 'tis the best place for a witch of a girl like her." She slumped with a puzzled look on her face and I called one of the serving girls to escort her to her bed.

There was not time enough to do more. I decided to walk back to my ship and retire to my own hammock on board. Strangely, the sounds and smells of a first rate man o' war, even the ship's bell and the bosun's calls, were a great comfort to me. I decided then to enlist the help of Ned in seeking what had caused Meg's desire for a meeting.

Some delay due to the rout was certain, and I assumed they were inevitable in the life of a spy – days of anguish, attendant on the doings of others, while lives were at stake.

Some of the matters decided at the lord lieutenant's abode were of direct concern to my story, but, as Ned oftentimes impressed upon me, the dabblings of our agents in the affairs of foreign kingdoms, were not to be spoke of.

There was an absolute need for silence on my part for the sake of the agents, indeed for the whole people of England, especially since dire events were forecast in the next weeks and months, he thought.

However, what transpired in the passage of time is now known to Britons generally, the great plans having now come to pass and bruited abroad, through the strivings of journalistic scribblers.

Ned's role at the admiral's rout was to take charge of a guard of stalwart sailors, disguised as waiters, and footmen. They duly escorted Black Dick round the guests, serving drinks for those to whom the admiral was to be introduced. The two senior admirals in the fleet, also made tours as a diversion.

The lord lieutenant was also closely involved in brief appearances in the reception rooms – what was known as 'window dressing.' As the party reached its climax those invited to attend the conference, numbering less than a dozen, I believe, repaired to a closely guarded cabinet at decent intervals.

This farrago was due to the activities of Rabouillet and Malfort. Ned claimed the affair of the *Paynton Rose* had caused severe embarrassment to Lord Howe.

"They had planted that bilge rat, Usher, amidships in Back Dick's inner staff, as his flag lieutenant." He chuckled at their boldness. "And, worse, they damn near got alongside of the King hisself in mid-Channel."

He shook his head in amazement, "Tis no wonder that naught was said about missing signal codes. Nor about that damn cutter, *Paynton Rose*. She was taken one night by Rabouillet and a cutting out party – Froggies to a man, I'll wager. The Devon crew come to light in someone's seine nets months later – they had weights round their ankles and their throats cut. We know that Rab, the skipper, had got 'isself a proper Devon man's lingo. I reckon e' 'imself was a fisherman, born and bred, from 'is 'andling o' the Rose."

He described the holding of the Grand Rout in one place, as an excuse for all the bigwigs concerned.

"'Twas commonsense to have it all over an' done damn quick – afore the buzz spread over, as it would with separate meetings with the Navy office, the Army and others, making it a very public country-wide business. Then, there's Usher and this Rab an' all the Frogs wot 'angs around Pompey. The ladies and gentlemen guests enjoyed the spread, unawares they were forming a useful cover for the back room."

Sir Charles Middleton of the Navy Board informed them at the 'backroom' meeting of the support for the fleet that he had put into being, while Sir Josiah Probyn sketched the situation in France, where the anxiety was to ward off starvation due to the levy of peasants for the Armies. Many farms were derelict. They were relying on corn to be shipped from America in a convoy of near 120 merchantmen, assembling across the Atlantic, and waiting escort to France.

Now it seemed the French fleet was turning to 'fireships' to escape the Channel fleet's blockade. By concentrating in Torbay, our fleet would be in a nearer position to observe the effect of our own blockade and to contain or intercept an invasion fleet under Admiral Villaret. French armies were also mustering to take ship to either England or Ireland, and a senior soldier from the Horse Guards office gave proposed movements of troops to the west country.

All this information became apparent later, when it had become known by the public, though I have thought to insert it at this stage to form a background of the events to come.

CHAPTER 14

After a day of struggling with my perplexities, I arrayed myself in seaman's shore-going clothes, having changed at the George in some secrecy. It was a scant disguise for I was known well enough at my destination. I was bound for the Golden Cross to answer Meg's enquiry for me.

I found Meg readily enough from the description given, for her appearance stood above that of the normal run of a barmaid, and did not match Doll's sour remarks. She was older than I had imagined, having been married to the agent for a minor aristocrat in Normandy. Her husband had had too close an acquaintance, I was told, with the town square guillotine in Dinan. The Committee of Securité had objected to his description of its members as "a pack of filthy layabouts who ape the aristocrats of France in their laziness."

Although his farm, or rather that of his former master, lay a good distance to the east, his wife Meganne had decided to sample the hospitality of the English before any connection was made between her and an outspoken peasant, executed in Dinan's walled town

Monsieur le Baron had suffered the same fate, but under a different guillotine, and Meganne had arranged the flight of Madame la Baronne, and attached herself as maid and children's nurse. But English hospitality did not extend to the whole of Madame's flock, and Meganne found herself catching the eye of Mr Fellowes, a wounded English sailor, who took her on as his farm partner, for she was indeed an expert as a maker of butter and cheese, as well as an excellent housekeeper and nurse. They settled in Hampshire in a state of platonic bliss.

Meganne – or 'Meg', as she became known – had improved the trade in the snug bar of the Golden Cross, where her command of English was excellent, and she quickly learnt what sort of discourse appealed to the tars and 'snotties.' Its attraction doubled when delivered heavily accented with French.

I quickly saw which way the wind blew and was struck by her dark eyes set in a Norman complexion, an alluring mixture. She was highly painted, and the sailors flocked to buy their drinks at her bar.

She was not at all flustered when I introduced myself in a casual way, asking if she wanted to speak with me; she replied without any attempt at beguilement – our business was on a different level, and she poured drinks for me and herself – to an astonished stir all round. I was glad to be wearing slops of a common hand in that bar.

Interest grew in our discourse as it grew closer, and I cannot deny a certain air of smugness that swept over me. Meg stepped aside for a word with another girl, coming back immediately, to whisk me away so deftly, that the growing dissent at the interfering manners' of an outsider faded as the street door swung shut behind us.

Outside Meg slipped her arm through mine, "to give a matrimonial pretence, not often seen in these parts except on occasions that are genuine, you understand."

I could not deny that her accent had a French tone that was slight, but attractive, to my senses and my arm pressed against Madame's a little more firmly.

Before I bethought me to enquire of where we went, she murmured, "M'sieur André, I have so wish to meet you – but we can discuss affairs better in my lodgings, yes?"

Oh yes, I thought with fervour.

We had reached an avenue of houses built for wealthier

people and she turned into one of three storeys, of which she had the uppermost.

Her eyes raked over me, seeming to discount my seaman's clothing, and, taking my hand to her lips she kissed it lightly, so that I seized hers in return and carried it to my lips, mumbling, "Enchanté, mam'selle." It was a stroke of genius – pure copy work from observations made on earlier occasions.

Her laughter tinkled and we found ourselves seated together on a small settle before a fire of coals.

Meg fetched wine from an adjoining room, and we settled to drink a little before we came to business. I was still in doubt, avid to discover her reasons for meeting – but not too hastily, I prayed.

After a second glass apiece, I found that Meg had no intention to put it off any longer, but murmured, "that can wait till later mon cher."

With a pounding heart I suffered greatly from my lack of perception – what could wait?

Meg turned her eyes on me and I felt hypnotised by their brilliance. "You know of a man whose name begins with 'P', "she began, and I nodded.

"Mister Probyn? Did he send you?" I blurted forth.

Meg shook her head. "It is not Mr Probyn," she chided me. She was confirming my identity, I supposed.

I thought fiercely – "Ah, Sir Josiah, the plant man?"

She nodded in relief. "One cannot be too careful. Do you know of someone in the region of Fecamp in Normandy?"

I nodded and felt relaxed. "Yes, but not his name or whereabouts. Sir Josiah, whose lodging is at the Keppel's Head here, knows him well and his place."

She smiled. "No more, cheri, it is sufficient."

She rose. "I will make a little repast, if you wish – you have leave to stay the night?" Her voice was gently teasing. "Sir Josiah says it is arranged."

Had I been 'arranged' too, I wondered.

I coloured red, and, nodded breathlessly. It was the start of a night that is imprinted in my mind for ever, as though I had been a virgin before and I felt guiltily that my will was seduced once more, as if by a first lover.

Before I departed in the early light of dawn, it came to me that the object we had discussed was the rescue of Jenny, somewhere in France. Meg knew it too but kept her counsel.

As if that was ignored by both of us as of no account, I had taken the word of a naked stranger that I would accompany her across the Channel to challenge the wiles of Usher and Rabouillet, without leave from my superiors.

A sense of disloyalty flowed over me. It would take some explaining to Mr Shaw in the cold light of day.

I took the boat from the steps on Portsmouth Hard, conscious that I was under the eyes of everyone who had permission to take that boat regularly to the Spithead, and, realising that I had taken the word of a barmaid, I had to stiffen my resolve to avoid being regarded as a credulous fool before all those familiar faces. I was certain they were all re-assessing me as an adulterer.

My enquiries at the gangway for Lieutenant Bashem were met with blank stares. Had I not heard? Mr Bashem was in the Naval hospital at Haslar. Soon everyone was at pains to inform me.

There was no news of Ned's whereabouts – he was just marked 'ashore' at the gangway, where I was told to report to Mr Shaw, the ship's master.

"Miller," he barked, "you are on your travels again, are

you? At any rate, I have been ordered to direct you to the Keppel's Head, where you are to report to this Sir Josiah Probyn – and to jump to it."

He surveyed me solemnly. "And for the love of God clean out of those damn deck-scrubbing slops, before you go ashore."

He shook his head. "Watch your step, young man, I want you back safely to finish making a navigator out of you." He waved me away and returned to his charts.

Some instinct made me pack a canvas bag for travelling, and the gangway staff had been warned to call a boat to row me back across the Solent.

And so to the Keppel's Head, where I was welcomed by Sir Josiah in his rooms, and, to my surprise I found Ned and Meg there. My companion of last night gave but the slightest sign of recognition, a coy smile, but it was lost on neither Sir Josiah nor Ned, due, thought I, to them having years of practice in observing of signs. Inwardly I was furious for allowing myself to blush.

Probyn could be brusque at times, and he commenced by baldly stating our immediate plans. "Madame has kindly consented to arrange a passage to Fecamp under the auspices of the gentlemen of Romney Marshes. She was certain they can equip us with a four-wheel cart of some sort. My contribution is of lambs, butchered as they prefer on the other side, which the Romney Marsh men can sell. That will be our fare, but they will expect us to barter for a share in their imports of wine and I will certainly cover that."

He broke into a hoarse chuckle and claimed that he was adept at the sport of smuggling in southern England, for which the outbreak of war was responsible in great increases of contraband trading across the Channel.

The journey started at a good pace after a meal in private at the inn. A post chaise rattled us along at a cracking pace, with only three or four changes of horse. Ned and I were supplied with appropriate clothing for our mission out of Sir Josiah's hamper of disguises. I could see his delight in the matter of dressing-up.

We were to play the parts of beggars or gypsies in Meg's part of Normandy.

We made our rendezvous with the Romney smugglers, the marsh men, as they preferred to be known, after a long wait in an isolated ale house, where Meg was already known. Our call came after midnight and began with a trek through marshland tracks accompanied by shadowy figures in anonymous black, unrecognisable at any future meeting. They spoke seldom, and when they did their language seemed foreign to all of us

I could not tell where we embarked, but the sea was surging over the beach, waist high, and I seized Meg to carry her to the pitching boat. It was well received, even by the marsh men and I was rewarded by Meg's close embrace and a whisper of thanks.

We scrambled into the waiting ketch and weighed her anchor, which started us on hours of hard pulling. Ned and I offered to take spells which prompted the silent men to pass round bowls of prawns in a hot gravy. There were periods of sailing too, whenever the wind served.

Our landfall in France had been visible for hours, but as the sun went down, we anchored off, amongst a number of others who acted as fishing vessels. Indeed, most were, for it was useful to bribe the French watchers ashore with a catch of fresh caught fish.

This levy was passed by our boatmen, and gained us an introduction on shore to the contact we were seeking, and soon we were possessed of a small gypsy caravan and horse, as had been agreed. From that point Sir Josiah took charge, and steered us by inland routes to his agent, outside Fecamp.

The darkness still prevailing, only Probyn was allowed to see this man who, we understood, went through life as a peasant recluse, isolated by a barrier of stinking heaps of dung and rotting vegetables. Probyn soon returned from the old friend of his youth, bearing a freshly drawn map of Rabouillet's hide-out, marked with the routes and guard points to be avoided as we got near.

Our little cavalcade got under way at once. It was essential, his agent had insisted, for he lived in mortal fear of a new force in France, called 'the police'. By daylight we had reached a deserted beach and embarked on netting scores of little silver fish – a delicacy in these parts, claimed Probyn.

This day we saw few passers-by, and stopped only to refresh our party and the horse. On our way we increased our stock of provisions by trade with passing pedlars, a little fishing and some poaching of game birds. Progress was still at a goodly pace, taking turns to eat and sleep in the caravan without stopping.

By evening Probyn was satisfied we were close to our night's destination and, after dark, we moved into a dense copse to feed and rest the horse and ourselves. While Ned and Probyn cooked, Meg readied our provision to make a display and, before we slept, we made ourselves up as pedlars.

We anointed our faces and limbs with dark stain and fitted cheap rings in our ears and coloured beads to our necks. My greatest reluctance was occasioned by the oils which Meg rubbed into my fair hair, but she did so with my head in her bosom, and I ceased from demurring.

"Pray do not be over-zealous in washing the dirt away," she giggled at her three men.

Before we slept, Sir Josiah took me to the edge of the nearby town. He gave me his time-piece, and directed me to rest at a large milestone, where I was to wait. "This bottle of cognac, in small doses, will keep your spirits up and the cold out," he chuckled, before disappearing in the shadows to meet with conspirators in the town.

If he had not returned at midnight by the pocket watch, said he, I was to return and tell the others he was captured. We would then withdraw to a little cove marked on our map and make signals to seaward. These, he expected, would bring a boat to take us off the beach and return us to England.

"With the blessing, Andrew, this may not be necessary, but, believe me, it is most disheartening to be without a plan of retreat."

At the eleventh hour he returned, evidently satisfied.

We were on the road early enough, after being schooled in our plan of action by Sir Josiah.

It was necessary to tempt Usher and Rabouillet out of their den, an old fortress, used now by the Police Brigade. He had learned that every week there were prisoners to be executed and our two enemies would accompany the tumbril conveying them. Their object was to hazard money at cards in the gaming room of a small inn at the scene of the executions. A fever for gambling was as great as their passion to attend at Madame Guillotine's gala performance.

As Probyn unfolded his ideas, Ned and I paid solemn attention, while it was plain that Sir Josiah himself and Meg revelled in every word with delight. It became crystal clear to me that Meg had done it all before, and that she was as much a spy as Probyn, her master.

Had she had been sent to recruit my services – to reel me into the network of spies? She must have known I was very willing to risk my neck to set Jenny free – I needed no coaxing. Both knew that I had sought out Meg at the Golden Cross myself.

In Breton sunshine, I stumbled along, leading the horse and feeling surly. It seemed that Meg really loved me. But I could never be sure and I felt obsessed with rescuing Jenny – my feelings were being torn in two directions.

At least the horse was happy, for our wheeled display stand was much lighter to pull than the caravan.

Then, pointing up the steep hill ahead, a sign directed us to Dinan.

We found people setting out their wares in the town market under a brilliant morning sun that glinted off turret and battlement. The raised square lay surrounded by tall houses and Meg led us to a pitch to one side of a small tavern. She was bent almost double, a wiry old woman with a heavy stick, her lank grey tresses blown about her face. A worn red shawl draped her shoulders and she shook as if with age and infirmity.

A side street, villainously cobbled, plunged steeply downhill from the square's side, and we moved our sales cart to its top corner. Ned and I sauntered towards it from the little tavern, carrying jugs of ale and cider. Ned muttered to Meg softly. "They're there in the backroom to the right. Dark red coats – no pistol in sight."

At the square's centre stood a raised platform supporting the soaring pillars of the guillotine. Carpenters hoisted the heavy blade, and the crowds gazed in morbid fascination, as did the prisoners in the open-air pen before the platform, where they awaited the machine's attentions. Other prisoners sprawled on the verges of square's edge, some weeping, some distracted with strong drink or with fear, their neck chains tended by armed guards.

One such group of three youths had been indicated by Probyn as those from Rab's police barracks, and we conversed quietly with their elderly guard. Yes, he was agreeable, the more so at the sound of the jingling leather pouch, surreptitiously shaken.

The warden looked up warily, as we stall-holders handed round the mugs – a kindly 'last gesture' to his three charges. His shaking hands held the chains to the leather collars round the prisoners' necks. He stared anxiously at our stout cudgels, and held out his hand for another mug, muttering fiercely that we were not to lay it on too heavy – he was quite au fait with shamming the unconscious.

Ned nodded and joked in immaculate French with him and his charges, over the beer and cider.

"Under yon table and downhill to the first gate to the left, friends – the guillotine will weep to lose your scrawny necks, hein?"

"And be quick about it, lads. There's no second chance with 'Madame Guillotine', hey?" He nodded to centre of the square, adding "and run like hell!" The youngsters grinned shakily into their mug, knowing by now that they must exert themselves.

He pointed to Meg. "And that one is a friend – do as she says, and you'll be free tonight."

The boys shook with fright as they gazed spellbound at the bent old dame, who squeezed round the corner to stump down the side street and out of sight. I collected their mugs and went to refill them at the tavern – boys' beer only this time, I thought. Ned had succeeded in reaching a deal with them. Across the square I could see Probyn herding some loutish youths into an alley between the tall stone houses, returning to the entrance to watch for our signals,

The opportunity came as the masked headsman mounted the platform, and the excited crowd pressed forward. Probyn knew that Usher and Rab were in the tavern's gaming parlour and, waiting only to see Ned's response, he retreated inside the alley, whence a crash of firearms volleyed forth, to set his gang shrieking and screaming, while from the prison pen rose a desperate chorus of groans. At this point Ned and I upset our table in the side street to form an obstacle to any chase there.

From then onward Probyn's schemes worked in smooth sequence, helped by the riot of the headsman's guard, who set about the crowd with clubbed muskets. Ned and I joined in the general fracas outside the tavern, shouting that the prisoners along the street were escaping.

Usher and Rab emerged at once, flourishing heavy pistols, in time to see the three lads stepping across their warden's limp form to clamber into the side street. The lads dallied at Meg's gate, long enough to entice Usher and Rab to pursue, while Ned and I followed unnoticed.

Meg and the boys were confronting Usher and Rab with pistol and club, and our enemies, I think, were about to surrender their arms, when we arrived and closed the gates behind ourselves. Then pent-up feelings exploded into action. Our two quarries were lost under a heap of bodies which hurled them to the ground. A flurry of fists reduced their calls for help to a mumble, and Ned produced some marline – a light line – to bind their arms.

After sunset our troubles were halved, the chief one being to recover our horse unnoticed. The riots had simmered down when Ned and I found him, still tethered, and we led him out of town, munching carrots, to where we had left the caravan and, after the horse was watered and fed, harnessed him for return.

After taking food and drink with us, the boy prisoners were set free on our way east from Dinan, and vanished in the darkness. As soon as they were out of earshot we bound the waggon wheels and set off in the opposite direction to the police barracks.

With Usher, tightly bound and gagged, as our guide, we manhandled him through passage and dungeon without great trouble, for he was at the mercy of Probyn, whose torture he had devised, there being no fraternal spark between them. My own hostility flared as we arrived at the prison cell of Jenny and her father. I found she had to tend the old man, night and day. It was not only from ill treatment however, but an infirmity due to old age, and fretting to re-visit the Karakoram mountains.

Jenny seemed not to know me at first but, after we extricated ourselves from the dungeons without interference, she grasped my arm, seeming only then to penetrate my disguise.

She had lost her voluble spirits over the old fellow, and I sensed he had little time left in this world. I had to restrain her from taking revenge on Rab and Usher, and her heavy knife was found and restored to her boot top.

"La, where is my sailor Prince," she scoffed. "Who is this common gypsy."

She tugged my tin earring, and rubbed my cheek painfully, as if to remove the dark dye.

I saw how troubled she was, and held my distance, for we could afford no falling out in the middle of Normandy with close-bound prisoners and a dying man. Probyn looked on stoically, with kind words for Jenny in her sorrow. Ned was distant, engaged in the double duties of scouting ahead, and keeping night watches with me.

At Fecamp, Probyn approached the lair of the agent of Admiralty, where he found the ramshackle den was wrecked, and when there was no sign of his old, troubled friend, he returned with the grim tidings.

"We must go into cover at once – away from here."

All agreed save Jenny, concerned as she was about moving her father in flight. She seemed on the verge of noisy dissent until Meg appeared, with a look of contempt on her face.

"I believe, ma'mselle, your father needs you," she spat, with unusual acidity in her voice.

Jenny turned round and sped to the old man's bedside. There was a short period of peace, followed by a sound of keening within the caravan, quickly suppressed, and Jenny reappeared, tears on her cheeks. She held out her hands to me, and I clasped her to me. Her father was gone, we understood.

Meg was visibly moved. She had helped in nursing the old man. "Your pardon, ma'mselle, for my unseemly outburst, it was at a tense moment for our safe progress... but a loss such as yours...!"

She trailed off, and, taking Jenny from my arms, drew her back to the old man's bedside once more. All we heard was soothing noises and a promise in Meg's low voice.

"I will stay with you to arrange things for your father – this is my country, you know." And the door closed.

We took flight to seek a hiding place near the beach used by the Romney men. Ned and I were required in the flagship at the Spithead, while Probyn was not and elected to stay with Jenny for her father's interment or cremation.

That left the question of moving our two prisoners to

England. The Romney men were likely to refuse passage, so Ned took over the problems of their custody.

In the wood where in good time we settled, he saw to the prisoners' meals, but kept them blindfolded at all times. To questions of where they should be left, he seemed vague and returned no clear answer.

At supper that night he left me to feed them, together with a bottle of strong spirit, as a parting gift. He said I was to lead them on strong tethers.

We toiled through a tangle of woodland to an old quarry working he had found.

"This 'ull do," Ned said, as he halted the prisoners and asked them to sit.

"I wish you a happy journey, mes camarades," he said and fumbled in his knapsack to extract another bottle.

Removing their blindfolds, he motioned to them, raising the bottle and sipping himself, as though toasting them.

He drank from it, and passed the bottle to me to tip to their lips. As they drank he looked oddly at me and told me to keep watch at the edge of the woods. I was gripped with icy panic and hastened into the trees to distance myself from the three of them.

I could not but guess at sinister intentions lying behind Ned's purpose in sending me away, for the land ahead, I knew, was rocky and water logged, with no place to keep watch for intruders. Ned himself had looked stricken and though I recognised him for past villainies, he had never before appeared so evil.

I waited in the woodland. Suddenly through the dense trees came two pistol shots.

As I ran back to the scene, I saw Ned before a deep quarry hole, standing as if dazed. I looked in and saw the two prisoners' bodies lying limp and bloody at the bottom.

"Pitch them boulders down, lad," he said wearily.

He intoned like a village parson. "Commit your bodies to the deep and to our comrades safety, and a speedy return."

I was shocked into silence, though there was no trace of mockery in Ned's voice, which made me fear Ned for the first time.

"Come, mate. They'd ha' done no better of a court martial. Pitch them boulders arter them."

Gritting my teeth, I complied.

Meg came to parley with the Romney men, for Ned and myself, and for Probyn and herself at a later day. She said naught of Jenny's intentions, but took me aside on the pretext of collecting firewood. At least that was her stated object, but she took me by the arm and pulled me close to her – within whispering distance.

"So that was your secret, my handsome," she murmured in a small bubbling voice. "Would you dally with me, sir? I perceive you are no stranger in the paths of love. But I make no wonder of it, for she is perfectly lovely, and she has confessed your affair."

Meg made a rueful grimace. I trembled but I thought her concern false. Why I should feel like a school lad discovered in his first amour, I knew not. I was unsure if this woman of the world toyed with me.

"Oh, Andrew," she commenced. "Jenny knew at once what occurred between us. A gypsy of her race is quite able to read hidden minds, and between storms of grieving for her father, she forgave me at least. She still holds you in her heart, sir."

Tears were shining in her eyes, and I held my council.

She took my head between her hands and looked deep in my eyes, until at last she sighed, and kissed me chastely on the lips. She was a skilled courtesan with a history of older lovers and I knew then that she was not for me and felt strangely relieved.

"Jenny is yours, Mr Miller, but you must fight to persuade her so – no, not with me, for I stand no chance against that one. You must persuade her so. Soon she will comprehend that the Karakorams, without her father to introduce her to the tribe and its wild lands, will not be enough without you – I feel it in every bone of my body.

"Besides there is my old man too. Josiah is fond of me, and I of him, he has told me so. Oh! Good Lord, would I make a master spy – the calling has its fascination, sir? La, do you watch your step, I think he sees me as 'Lady Probyn' – when this war is over. Old gentlemen of England cherish the idea of taking a Frenchwoman to bed, especially one of discretion."

All the time she giggled, and, still laughing, turned to gather sticks.

PART 4 – THE CLASH OF FLEETS

CHAPTER 15

Our passage to the Kentish coast was meticulously arranged by Meg and our relations with the Romney Marsh men were made smoother by their recognising that we – Ned and I – were seamen too. Meg's skill in organising extended to the post-chaise journey to Portsmouth, where we encountered a very different atmosphere.

Ned and I arrived at last on board the fleet flagship, where we did not need to be told that something great was afoot. The very air on Portsmouth Hard spoke of a sharp turn of events.

Behind the main gate, the dockyard was buzzing like a hive of bees, even the dray horses seemed to have found a gait faster than dawdle, and – wonder of wonders – Ned did not even look to an hour in the George.

The Spithead anchorage was even more a pell-mell, particularly at the ammunition buoy, where the hoys, all flying the red danger flag, lay off, like an angry parcel of bees, each awaiting her turn alongside. Many more were at the Gun Wharf inside the harbour proper, soon to, emerge sated to make a place for the next man.

As each squadron and division of ships of the line completed its feast of powder, it cleared the Spithead under its divisional rear admiral, gave the customary salutes to the fleet commander and vanished, bound for Plymouth or Torbay.

Ned made his report to the boatswain, and I to the master. Mr Shaw greeted me with an air of weary resignation.

"Very good, Miller. I am not allowed to enquire, but I hope it was a profitable picnic. I mean of profit to his Majesty, of course!"

His next words showed that even officers had access to their own scuttlebutt.

"Was it not remiss of you and that well-connected bosun's mate to leave your principal ashore – ahem – over the water? And where are the prize fillies, hey? I hear that Sir Josiah has inclinations towards the gentle sex! Ah! I do believe the lad blushes." He roared with delight.

"Mr Hector Collins has need of your services, this instant. 'Tis great pity you have not thought of him in the matter of smugglers' bottles. We are stocking up our lockers for a long spell, look you. But you'll learn, you'll learn."

What I learnt was that he had a fruity chuckle.

Another two days of work on the guns and magazines, the rigging and the victualling, passed before the Centre Squadron was 'topped up', as they say, and ready to sail for the west. The first division, led by *Gibraltar*, 80 guns, left the mooring followed by the *Queen Charlotte*, 100 guns.

The Centre Squadron, second division, followed under the command of Rear Admiral Gardner. But I digress, since the formation of the British and French lines of battle are set down in an appendix at the rear of these memoirs, on pages 200 and 201.

We occasionally caught the sounds of the Blue Squadron at gunnery practice astern, which told us that the Rear Squadron of the line was at sea and formed.

The good folk of England's South coast must have wondered, as county after county resounded to a continuous cannonading on their seaboard, thunderclap after thunderclap rolling forth, as in the days of their ancestors down the ages. The sound came uneven on the blustering winds against which the fleet made wide tacks to make headway towards Start Point.

On passage I had not seen hair nor hide of Jemmy Bashem, nor indeed since returning from Normandy. Then in one boisterous middle watch, the officer of the watch, our third, feeling inclined for a little conversation, I guess, reminded me I had been on 'cutting-out parties' with the fourth, though I had avoided going into any detail with him.

"Damn'd hideous luck to befall our Jemmy, ain't it?" says he, and it flashed upon my mind that the last I had heard of Jemmy Bashem, was of him being in hospital at Haslar. I was not to find out any more just then, for a bitter squall smote us abeam and laid us over somewhat, causing the third to spring to the helm to peer into the lighted binnacle at our compass heading.

The rain rattled on my tarred hat, half deafening me, but I made out his order to call the master and the captain and tell them that sail needed shortening. The watch below was being piped on deck as I went to do his bidding.

The next hours were spent aloft, clewing the main and mizzen topsails. It was but a moderate gale that we struggled with, and we won our round, scudding to windward without great mishap, save the scattering of our formation. The sea was covered with lights which rose and fell, vanishing and re-appearing in all directions. As the flagship, we showed our toplights and called attention to them by means of signal guns, from time to time.

It was a relief to sight the great lantern at the Start as dawn struggled through the clouds and the wind tailed off to reveal Mr Bowen swaying against the still-lively motion like some amiable giant. He fixed his eye on me.

"Ah, 'tis young Miller, is it not? Are you come to take charge of the quarter deck, lad?"

"Not I, Mr Bowen," I touched my cap. "Main and mizzen topsails made fast sir. Am I to set them again?"

Bowen turned to the flag captain and they laughed together in the light of the rising sun. "Oh, a master's mate, is he now?" Bowen marvelled, turning his beaming face my way, and winking hugely.

The low coastline moved past us to larboard until we had Berry Head on the beam, and Torbay caught the dawn's rays, a picture of peace and serenity – for a while.

We remained outside the little harbour to come to a single anchor off the town. The seas had gone down enough for the victuallers and hoys, together with a variety of other tenders, to refill our holds and magazines again, so depleted by our days crowded of gun practice.

Some of the victualling ships, it seemed, were to accompany the fleet towards Brest to re-stock us at sea, to replace further depredations, for a long haul was expected investing the French arsenal at its 'land's end.'

There was to be soft tack and Plymouth beer, and fruit and greens too, against the scurvy. We heard that we were also to have beef on the hoof, already arrived to judge by the anguished bellowing that rent the air. The hospital ship, *Charon*, and a fireship, *Incendiary* made up the fleet's train of tenders. A long haul expected indeed.

The mailbag had not caught up with our shifts of berth and I shrugged off any expectations of news from Jenny or Meg, nor even news from Broadwell.

Sir John Blunder's man of the law had evidently none to impart either.

Ned contrived to have words with me in the dogs that day. His despatching of our two enemies, Usher and Rabouillet, by summary pistol was preying on his mind, I suspected, leading to a grim outburst that was markedly unusual in him.

"Oh aye, I had to pitch my tale to the flag captain, and then to Black Dick 'isself. I explained to them the 'ole we was in, with a dying Romany on our slop chit and a passage over the channel to be got under way. Sir Probyn and that Meg was sartain they must bide with the gypsy gel, but would come over when possible. Neither the admiral nor the flag captain seemed to know why the wimmen was in it an' I thought it best not to enlighten them.

"Their chiefest concern seemed to be not to lay open such confidences in public at a court martial.

"I told 'em I weren't fer takin' any chance with them Froggie murderers by bringin' them over to justice – they got justice awright in that wee bitty quarry, I reckons. It 'ould be out anyway if we tried to pass them off on the marsh men.

"With you, mate, 'twas different – I brought it upon your shoulders with never a word o' what was to 'appen. You stood fast by me – I explained that – so it's naught to do wi' you, Mister!"

He clapped me on the back and turned heavily away.

I knew he was sincere – not a trace of the 'old rogue' was there. Though a spasm of anxiety ran through my guts, I returned his back-slap right hearty. "Did they accept it?"

"Aw, too right they did. Black Dick shook me by the hand and said I did right. The flag captain, he just nods. It would not surprise me if he warn't thinkin' of all the to-do that came of Usher escaping from ship's cells that morning in Pompey, eh?

"Well there ain't no risk o' that, any more," says he.

I took the occasion to enquire if there was any news of how Bashem fared and, as always, he had the latest events at his fingertips.

"Aye. It seems our Jemmy is in deep water. He was leading his boarding party up the side o' this East Indiaman, to enter any volunteers for the Navy, but – this time – the skipper, a ravin' Jock from Glasgow, warn't about to dance to our Jemmy's tune. The boarding port was blocked up and a gang o' Lascars of 'is crew began showering our hands with heavy rocks. Two Charlottes was knocked off the ladder and swept away on the tide.

"Well Jemmy just dives in and pulls one out, but nary a one in the *Defence* boat seems to think it's their part of ship to join in the rescue – the scum – and our second man's swep' away.

"Jemmy rallies 'is lot and they swarm up the side, banging off their guns whenever a head shows o'er the rail. On the deck, our muskets still pointing, the lascars could see it's all up, and throws down their pikes, but their skipper charges our lads on 'is own, waving a bloody great Scotchman's sword and yelling war cries. That were a sight I'll wager.

"He nearly reaches Jemmy with this sword – it's double the usual length, but our corporal o' marines sticks a foot out an' trips him, I hear. Unluckily the point of the great blade scores Jemmy all down his side – fair deep, and Jemmy goes down spouting blood through his clothes.

"This corporal's an old timer – seen Indian service, I think – and he catches Jemmy and staunches the blood mighty quick, shouting instructions to 'is men all the time. I reckon 'e saved our orficer's life, and routs out a good number o' hands for the press into the bargain.

"They was hiding in small dens or cuddies and double skins built into the ship's sides, even the deckheads. The crafty so'jer tells his Jollies to search the ship for sawdust an' shavings on the deck, then smash open any new timberwork. They had a good haul, all prime deep-sea men. They was all white men at that, and heading for hearth and home with a good load of Far Eastern loot.

"The skipper o' the Indiaman is put in irons, but no sooner'n they set foot on shore, than a sly agent is trying 'is best to stick a writ on Jemmy for attempted murder, as he goes by on his stretcher – and again on our flag captain for 'habeas corpse'.

"All is 'ushed up till they says they'll bring charges agin the admiral – just as he sails on this 'ere banyan. I don't think we'll hear a word from the penny-snatching legal men till Black Dick is back in 'arbour."

The flagships of squadron divisions were kept busy with convoy work, all the time a-coming and going from Torbay. So much so that I wondered if all our merchantmen were permanently kept at sea, making hay while the French trade was arrested – kept in harbour by our blockading ships.

Already the journals and pamphleteers had christened him 'Lord Torbay' for not being at sea. Although our commander-in-chief was known not to favour tying up his sail of the line at blockade work, we now expected to be on the trail of the enemy, not tied up in port, at instant notice. He was worried about delays by the dockyards in repairing storm damage to our line of battle.

Before long however it seemed our time had come to depart when a swarm of boats appeared from Torbay's inner harbour making for our larboard gangway.

"Ah, the missing 'bullocks', I presume," came the voice of Mister Shaw at my side. Bullocks, lobsters, jollies – I understood the several nicknames of our sea-borne soldiers, and peered through my telescope, which I carried as mate of the watch.

My eye was dazzled by the scarlet coats and the gleaming white of the pipe-clayed belts of the 'marines', for that would be their designation once they were on board, a whole company of them, settled in their 'barracks', as they would be taught to call their mess, aft.

The legend had it that they were placed there to protect the ship's officers, from riotous lower deck men. They would certainly have to adapt to sea-going life, I thought.

"Pretty ain't they?" Mr Shaw continued. "I believe they're from the Queen's Royal Regiment of Foot, so keep an eye open for them. Ah! especially that be-medalled and be-sashed fellow with the whiskers. He's the sergeant major, I believe. Don't run him in, and charge him for not shaving. I believe he's rated a warrant officer," he paused... "same as me, I suppose, only a different warrant. I warn you, he'd probably make a meal of you – you have enough sauce!"

Mr Shaw's pearls of wisdom ceased there for I had to go to the starboard gangway, where another, more sumptuous boat, was in the offing.

"Alright, Mr Miller," grinned the officer of the watch, "No need for extreme measures, this one's the company officer of the bullocks, I see – not rated for a side party if I do not mistake it, nor a pipe from the bosun's mate."

He peered at the boat, where an officer in gleaming regimentals stood becloaked in the stern-sheets, seemingly unimpressed by a flagship, though Captain Hamlet had had the grace to appear, and was taking a stance to greet the new-comer.

"Sword and dirk, if you please, gentlemen, our new bullock is of field rank, I fancy, and will surely be hefting a damn great sabre up the gangway."

He peered quickly through his telescope, as the officer of the watch signalled 'no pipe' to the bosun's mate.

The boat was hooked on to the bottom of the steps and a short spring delivered the newcomer into the side boy's helping hand, but he shrugged it aside and appeared on deck without delay, doffing his laced hat. He was revealed to me, in all his glory, as Major Richard Blunder, my father, whose face tightened at the sight of me.

My mind was reeling. I had never foreseen sharing a ship with my father. If he was taken aback, he quickly recovered, and turned half left to stamp and click his heels in a soldier's salute to the quarter deck. With a bow he shook hands with the captain. The watch keeper and I saluted him and he was whisked away to meet the C-in-C.

"He seems pleasant enough for a bullock," noted Ogilvey, the officer of the watch. "No doubt we'll see his form as a mess-mate in the wardroom."

Ogilvey's laugh was like a braying ass, and I wondered what prompted it. In no time I was to learn.

"We had another candidate yesterday, a protégé, I believe, of Black Dick."

He looked about him to see if he was overheard.

"A friend o' the Howe family, I gather, very unusual. He's a new midshipman, straight out of the bandbox, though he is aged twenty three – to be allowed the privileges of the wardroom, by Jove!

"Name of Codrington, and over a fathom high – more than six feet from truck to keel. Black Dick is said to treat him like a son, his family being all gels, you know." There he stopped abruptly, for the first lieutenant was bearing down on us with orders to pipe round the ship to prepare for weighing by two bells in the dogs.

I took the opportunity to break away from the garrulous Ogilvey. But as the new watch keepers relieved us, I raked over recent events as I made my way to the gunroom mess, not, it seemed, to be graced by the six-foot midshipman, who was to be under the charge of the master – my part of ship.

Most likely we were going to sea for a long haul and there was no chance of visiting Jemmy Bashem at Portsmouth, scant chance of mail and less chance of learning the fate of Jenny or Meg, unless Probyn renewed his habit of turning up anywhere at the least convenient time.

Would I hear from the Blunders? My mother certainly knew of my ship, and grandfather, Sir John, too. I wondered if he or his legal man might correspond from Broadwell. It was almost certain that Eleanour would, I told myself.

The fleet was at sea as one entity again, creeping cautiously in most indifferent visibility, there being occasional very steep seas, which slowed our progress considerably.

Despite all this, there was a buoyant sense of confidence on board, an expectation amongst all ranks and ratings to come up with the enemy. In the gun decks there was jesting and boasting, the hands relating the old axiom that "one British tar can thrash any three Frenchmen."

This was a firm gospel, but to the assertion that French ships were of better design, better built, under superior cordage and canvas, no one made much demur. Everyone knew there was swindling and idleness in our dockyards.

Some said that the Spaniard was even better at shipbuilding, in spite of which, there was no doubt that British gun drill and guts would win the day. The news of armies of French peasants sweeping away the best troops of Europe was known generally by the British public. That the Frogs might be inspired by a revolutionary fervour on the land was of no account to Jack Tar at sea.

It was known now that the French Admiral Vanstabel, had been in the United States some time with five sail of the line to escort the grain convoy back to France. Rear Admiral Neilly had another squadron of ships to patrol the convoy's approach to a home port in the Bay of Biscay. It was under orders not to seek out action, but if no other course presented itself, to protect the convoy at all costs.

So vital was the safe arrival of these precious ships than an official from the Ministry of Marine was to accompany the fleet to ensure that the French were victorious. The official was Citizen Bon-Jean Saint André – no sailor – but he threatened vicious reprisals if revolutionary fervour for victory was in any way lacking. He took a berth in the flagship, *Le Montagne*, 110 guns, whence he was said to harass everyone from admiral to powder boy, without ever appearing on deck when the guns roared.

Fortunately for the French, their fleet commander, Rear Admiral Villaret de Joyeuse, had developed a placid exterior to this governmental oppression. He had been an officer of the old regime, who escaped the guillotine, and remained in the fleet as a bosun, promoted to lieutenant and to rear admiral after the revolution.

In Howe's fleet there was a determination to bring them to a battle they had avoided twice the previous year.

CHAPTER 16

The Channel fleet had thirty four sail of the line when it sailed with a convoy of British merchantmen, the latter bound for Newfoundland and the Indies, West and East. Off the Cornish Lizard, eight sail of the line were detached under Rear Admiral Montagu as close escort to the convoy. They were to rejoin the fleet when their charges were abreast of Cabo Finisterra on the north west coast of Spain, and considered out of the danger zone.

Montagu's orders on leaving the British convoys were to patrol on a line in the Bay of Biscay designed to intercept the expected French grain ships before they reached their home ports. It was a considerably difficult task.

April had given way to May, but the weather appeared distinctly unlike May's usual reputation, and by the fifth we wallowed in a miserable fog. It was then we learned that *Orion* and two frigates had found the French fleet still in Brest.

Two French frigates were in Camaret Bay just to the south and a score of larger vessels in the Gullet, even closer to Brest harbour.

They looked ominously ready to depart, though, and Howe, wanting them at sea, cleared their path by sailing south west himself for seven days. By the 19th, his frigates reported that Brest was empty and fishing vessels declared that the Brest fleet had passed us in the fog, overhearing the pipes and drums of our ships.

The Atlantic traffic seemed to present a scene crowded with activity, and the weather was mostly bad. It was in just such a spell that a fishing vessel of the Newfoundland fleet, taken prize by Villaret's fleet, was re-captured and we learnt of the Frenchman's whereabouts and the course he held.

On May 25th two French corvettes were captured at night and burnt, since the British fleet lacked the prize crews to sail them home.

There were vessels of all sorts, for the Atlantic was awash with trade from the smallest fishing boat, little more than a cockler, to bustling merchantmen and packets of all sorts. Every watch it was "Ship ahoy – heave to. I am about to board you." Often it was the frigates who performed this task, and had to retail whatever news was gained to the Flag.

It was information from these sources that caused our admiral to alter the fleet's course and give chase to Villaret, instead of following Montagu and the convoys. By May 28th our frigates on the skyline were flying the signal for 'enemy in sight.'

Once again Mr Codrington – now promoted to lieutenant – earned his reputation for remarkable eyesight, when he hailed the quarterdeck with an accurate count of the French fleet at near ten nautical miles distance through mist and flying spray.

"Your opponents number twenty six of the line, sir," he cried, doffing his tarpaulin cap with a flourish. "Does this not amount to 'Even Steven?'"

"No, sir, it does not. Their guns outnumber ours and the Frenchman has a good deal greater weight in his broadside." He stumped off.

Mr Shaw, Codrington's new mentor, nodded after the admiral. "The admiral is right, Mr Codrington; the French have a good number of carronades, firing huge shot, fearful at short range. And pray remember that Black Dick does not relish advice of that sort."

I was on watch, when these words were uttered and could not help but notice Black Dick's gait as he stepped below – a little unsteady on his pins. I asked Mr Shaw if it was not more prudent to appoint younger admirals to such an active command as the Channel squadron.

"Miller, my boy, I have never had the honour to hear a speech like that from the Board of Admiralty until now. Your lordship may wish to know that there are but three admirals in the whole of our Navy with experience enough to handle such a fleet as this – and to fight such an enemy into the bargain! Congratulations, sir. I suppose you wish now to know the names of these paragons". He grinned most horribly before continuing.

"Why sir, they are my Lord Howe, Sir Alexander Hood and Admiral Graves," he said.

There ended my lesson in saying naught while keeping my eyes about me, for at that very moment a sing-song hail rang out that the enemy had disappeared into a fog bank. Aloft, I confirmed the lookout's accuracy, and slid below, where the new watch was being piped together with 'Hands to breakfast' for the remainder.

Mr Shaw was like a wise old owl, I thought, as we went our ways to our separate messes. "Mr Miller, the fleet, or part of it, might very well come to action today – and though I am not your hand maiden, might I advise a clean shirt and nether garments? The doctors say it does wonders in preventing wounds from turning bad."

As it turned out, five ships of the Van under Admiral Paseley in HMS *Bellerophon* saw the first action between Howe's and Villaret's fleets. After noon he was ordered to take stations for attack, and I noted that two flags only were required to pass that order. Paseley's 'flying squadron' bore the brunt of the day.

It was some nine or ten miles distant from our own main body of ships, and in the mist that prevailed we saw but little. However the continuing cannonade came to our ears at fitful intervals and caused excited speculation about our comrade's fortunes.

By evening on the 28th May, the French three-decker *Revolutionnaire* had had to fall out of their rear squadron, badly mauled. In failing light she and the British *Audacious*, 74, were forced to limp away toward their respective home ports.

These were but the preliminary skirmishes before the main engagement of line against line. To my amazement the enemy had lost five of her line permanently, and detached other ships to escort or take the wounded ships in tow. On a stormy night, the giant *Revolutionnaire* confirmed that she had struck her colours, but before daylight when we returned to take possession she had vanished.

Miraculously the French deficiencies were restored when later Rear Admiral Neilly appeared with five ships from his Biscay squadron. Admiral de Villaret's fleet again totalled twenty six of the Line, against twenty five British.

On the evening of the 30th May, with the two fleets standing westward, the weather grew thicker. They were more than nine miles apart, making very slow speed, and so the conditions remained with the wind at sou-west.

Howe's careful tactics to windward finally gained us the weather gage, wresting it from the French fleet. From now they could only escape downwind, leaving themselves open to our pursuit.

At last the fog cleared after noon on the 31st and I recall the relief of the ship's company to see the French on a like course to our own westerly. It was too late to engage that evening but, after a night of crowding on sail, we were finally poised to attack by ten o'clock on first of June.

The plan, which Howe had long preached, was for each ship to mark his opposite in the French line and to turn in towards him at the given signal. His intention was to break through the spaces in the enemy's line, to give raking fire into his stern and turn on him on his leeward side.

On the morning of the 1st of June, Lord Howe was finally satisfied of the two fleets' relative positions and ordered, "Hoist number thirty-four." In full it signified: 'Having the wind, the admiral intends passing through the enemy ships and engaging them to leeward.'

Then Black Dick was seen to smile and the news went round the ship. As always it was the understood custom of the British fleet to conform with the admiral's manoeuvres.

We closed the French line on an angled course, and the *Queen Charlotte* soon came under fire from ships astern of *Le Montagne*, making work aloft vastly more exposed than before.

The enemy's line spread imposingly on each side. The gap we aimed for at *Le Montagne*'s stern was unduly wide and Villaret was backing much sail to close it, while *Jacobin*, his next astern, was making more sail for the same reason. All was clamour now and thunderous broadsides rent the air around. In this bedlam I saw they were in danger of collision and the *Jacobin*'s only course was to escape to starboard, to leeward.

Howe steered into the space left, and fifty of our broadside raked through the full length of *Le Montagne*'s hull. It was said that 300 men were killed then, including Captain Bazir, the French flag captain. For a while she fell silent and our broadside fired on her starboard timbers. Almost simultaneously our ships struck the foe all along the line. French muskets poured fire over their bulwarks, creating havoc among our marines, and I caught a glimpse of the bearded sergeant major carrying one of his men below, trailing blood as he went.

I must stress the impossibility of seeing every melee which flared up almost simultaneously at every point of the line. Not wishing to press all the violent events upon the reader, I draw a veil over what was invisible beyond clouds of cannon smoke, and harrowing actions obscured from our eyes on board the flagship.

Only six of our ships broke Villaret's line that day, though many attacked them closely on their weather sides, but one encounter near the *Queen Charlotte* deserves a brief mention for its ferocity and resource on both sides.

The British ship *Brunswick*, our next astern, had collided with *Le Vengeur de Peuple*, both of 74 guns, trapping her anchor solidly in the Frenchman's rigging. So tightly embraced were they, side by side, that neither ship could open her gun ports until the British gunners blew theirs apart with gunfire and served their guns with flexible rammers and sponges.

On deck the Vengeurs were preparing to board, sweeping the *Brunswick*'s officers and men with deadly musket fire and langridge from their heavy carronades. Captain Hervey, wounded thrice, was taken below and later died. Down below the *Brunswick*'s gunners kept up a constant barrage, firing upwards and then downwards into the very fabric of *Le Vengeur de Peuple*.

At the approach of two British ships the boarding parties in *Le Vengeur de Peuple* had to man their guns on her disengaged side. Meanwhile *L'Achille* was returning to her aid. With only her foremast remaining, she came under fire from *Brunswick* who had mustered a few guns' crews from each of her gundecks. Their fire brought *L'Achille*'s remaining mast down, and effectively disabled her.

Now *Ramillies*, 74, commanded by the brother of *Brunswick*'s captain, came on the scene, and in a brief bombardment removed all of *Le Vengeur de Peuple*'s masts, before departing to take *L'Achille* prize.

Thankfully, the fight was nearly over when *Le Vengeur de Peuple* wrenched clear of her opponent's anchors but the shot-holes and the open ports were taking in water steadily. Her devoted crew fought to save her, by throwing her guns overboard, pumping and bailing. It was no good – *Le Vengeur de Peuple* was sinking steadily.

Nearly 400 of her men were rescued by boats from two British ships, who, overloaded, drew away from the sinking wreck, to the despairing sounds of the remainder of her company raising cries of 'Vive la Republique.'

All our boats that could swim were away from the ship and we could only watch helplessly. The sight of fellow mariners going to their graves was so affecting that tears started to my eyes, and many of my shipmates wept openly.

I heard the 'butcher's bill' in the *Brunswick* was forty-four killed and fourteen wounded, but that of the *Le Vengeur de Peuple* was not recorded.

The main action was over early in the afternoon, when the exhausted Earl Howe retired from deck. He had snatched naught but short naps in a chair since May 29th and handed the conduct of our fleet to Sir Roger Curtis, the first captain. In the evening a signal was made for ships to close on the admiral, and orders given to abstain from chasing, even to secure prizes.

Fourteen of our ships had been dismasted to some extent, and there was much work to do on the six

Frenchmen we had taken. Both sides suffered vastly from lack of mobility for days after the battle had finished.

It was then that I found Major Blunder had taken a ball in a vulnerable part of his abdomen. He was in the cockpit still and I hurried there to find him lying, white and prone, still on a blood-stained pallet. All my rancour towards him fled.

I had seen little of the major and only heard of his role as the senior marine officer from hearsay. To have a full company on board under the command of a major only fell to flagships. I believe he was addressed simply as 'soldier' by his equals in the wardroom. He had little to take him about the ship save to become familiar with the working of guns, for the marines manned several; but he was always to the fore in boarding practice and virtually led in shore landings, tho' under naval command.

Nows he lay lost to his senses, they said, and I was hurried out. My next concern was that mother would suffer, should he die, and I resolved on seeking her out.

The *Queen Charlotte* gave what cover she could to the fleet, sailing home with difficulty, without our fore topmast until we fetched up in Portsmouth, to be hailed as victors. Admiral Graves was wounded and remained at Plymouth.

Many of the French line had gone to leeward earlier and at last the crippled *Montagne* joined them to the north. We learnt that Villaret's remaining ships reached haven in Brest on 11th June, followed a few days later by Vanstabel's grain convoy, totally intact.

CHAPTER 17

From a rapturous welcome at first, the public reaction at Portsmouth soon became muted. I thought this might be due to the damaged state of many of our ships, which required dockyard repair, the *Queen Charlotte* especially because she was intended to act as host ship to the King and Queen. With rumours of a French invasion still rife, an overlong delay could not be contemplated, and some repairs and re-rigging was moved away from the Yard to be done by sailors.

Nevertheless, Jack Tar was content to swagger round the ale houses in a glow of self-satisfaction, though it might have been doubled if his prize money had been assessed without the burden of lengthy and expensive repairs.

Mr Shaw had volunteered my transfer to the rigging gangs, observing tartly that I would suit "that gang of monkeys."

He meant it kindly, I had no doubt, but it also meant no leave for home visits to Broadwell, and I was confined to letter-writing. Once more, I was fettered.

However there was no bar to visiting my father at Haslar, and Mr Bashem too, if he chanced to be there still, and boats for this purpose were easy to obtain. Thus I found myself being ushered into an officer's ward, and trapping two rabbits in one hole, to my immense pleasure.

The two men were sitting together at cards, and I noted towering piles of markers at the marine's elbow, as he added to their number with a guffaw at his companion's expense. Both men looked round at my entry and Bashem hailed me heartily.

I must confess I was at a loss to know how to address

my father, not least because I was unsure that he would acknowledge our relationship. I thrust forth my hand and greeted him warmly.

"How pleased I am to see you so improved, sir."

"Andrew, my lad. I have had many reports about you from my father, 'er – quite flattering. I do believe he is pleased with his grandson..."

He grew red with embarrassment.

"Will you go to see him at Broadwell?"

Saying I was obliged to stay with the flagship for the time being, I enquired diffidently about my mother. He looked grave as he told me she had only that morning returned to Plymouth to cope with her new baby's ailments.

"She will grieve not to have seen you, but I will write an express to tell her you are returned from the great battle, unscratched, as I trust."

Jemmy was now got to his feet, shaking me by the hand and demanding to know the details of our ship's doings. He shook his head and bemoaned his missing 'the banyan.'

"What the devil are we to call this battle?" he demanded. "It is way beyond the neighbourhood of Land's End, ain't it?"

I fished a scrap of paper I had carried from the ship out of my pocket and read out a position by latitude and longitude. "This was the centre of the battle," says I, "Just over 400 miles westward of Ushant."

"I'll wager that every man-jack on board is at odds for a name for our little encounter," grumbled Jemmy Bashem, still aggrieved over his absence from the battle. I nodded agreement.

"Why not name it for the day – the Battle of the First of June," offered my father. The notion was to be ascribed to

Jemmy – who should send it to the admiral's secretary, with a letter to the admiral in praise of his victory. It was to be signed by Jemmy, excusing his absence from the great day.

Major Blunder was eager to assist with the wording of it, in the hope of assuaging Jemmy's troubles with the law. I left them hard at it.

A dockyard rigger took over the re-rigging, with parties of ship's seamen to follow on with slushing down, tying new ratlins and painting, before the sail maker was ready for sending fresh canvas aloft. In most of these activities I had been heavily engaged.

At last I was able to pay a call on Doll's domain in the George Inn and made my way there, full of a renewed anticipation. I had not seen Ned for some time, I told the old trout, but earned only a sniff.

"Aw, me darlin' boy, 'tis poor news I have for yiz, an' all," she says, clutching me about the neck. "Didna yer sweet Ma, stand just where y'are standin' now? And her gone back to Plymouth, the pair o' you loike ships that pass in the night, I tell you."

We got no further for a strange event took place in the taproom bar that evening. It cast a light on how the local folk, longshoremen, porters and the like regarded men of the Navy, now that the first battle of fleets in this war had ended in victory for the Royal Navy after years of neglect.

It started when a complete stranger tapped me on the shoulder.

"Ahoy Jack!" cries he, hearty-like, "I hear you was with the Channel fleet, dusting off the monsoors – take this jug, lad, we drinks to you and your mates, coupled with the Lord Howe."

A cheer went up as Doll and I were surrounded by enthusiastic customers, many of them taking the opportunity to shake my arm off, or to kiss Doll as if she was but seventeen.

Soon there were beer mugs lined up on the bar as far as the eye could see and more toasting and cheering, hugging, and laughing together with mounting hysteria.

At the centre of the throng I caught glimpses of Doll's face, flushed with laughter. She raised both hands in resignation for her lost conversation but she was loving the clamour of it.

When the opportunity came I slipped away, and could not be spared for the next few days while the flagship was readied for the Royal visit. An ornately gilded royal barge was procured from the dockyard, for which a crew of ten oarsmen was to practise pulling. Every one was a captain in the Channel fleet, flushed with the honours awarded to them.

The Queen and her ladies were to accompany King George at Royal banquets on board the flagship and the ship hummed like a beehive with the preparations. We heard of gold medals, golden chains and promotions, ranging from peerages for Admirals Hood and Graves to baronetcies for commanders of divisions. Ned advised me not to expect leave to be absent from Portsmouth till all the celebrations were accomplished.

The first of my personal business, after a sheaf of letter-writing, was to call on Sir Josiah Probyn at his rooms. Over the inevitable glass of wine, the jovial spy-master put me at my ease by his brevity.

"I am delighted to report that your Romany lady is well

recovered and is prepared to settle in this country, should the attentions of a young master's mate be still pointed in her direction."

I leapt to my feet in an attempt to shake him by the hand, regardless of the large wine glass clutched there. He evaded my grasp easily, laughing with me at my clumsiness.

"I do thank you, sir," I burbled, partly giggling at my eagerness and partly choking with a sudden rush of tears.

"There, sir, I see I mistook your aptitude for joining that monstrous regiment, the collectors of secrets – your visage has no notion of controlling its feelings, which is a fatal failing for a spy. You are to be congratulated on such a respectable failing. A wise choice, sir."

With great pursing of his lips and shaking of his head, he thrust one hand toward me, while the other was lifting the decanter of wine. He was certain that Jenny would turn up but could not tell me her whereabouts.

I walked along the Hard as if floating on clouds, assuring myself that I could wait.

When I came to earth I decided to alter my course to the George Inn to renew my quest for Doll's news, for the place had become a centre for meetings second only to the Keppel's Head. I found her in the taproom, sitting by the blazing fireplace. She greeted me with her usual fussiness, first calling for a mug of ale for me. A slim figure brought the drink on a tray, approaching behind my shoulder. A cool hand descended to stroke my cheek and I was astonished to find it was Meg, bedazzling me once again with her brightness.

"Ah monsieur, welcome back."

She bent to kiss my burning face, and I marvelled that Doll made no objection. Apparently she had changed her opinion of Meg's character, for she clucked amiably.

"Madame is assistant housekeeper of the George now and takes all the cares and woes of this house from my shoulders," she smirked proudly. "Besides, I can keep my eye on her, when that rogue Ned Bowlin chances to call."

She wheezed with laughter behind her hand, and we all nodded furtively as if she was not audible to everyone within a fifty fathoms circuit.

The Frenchwoman was dressed in the height of fashion, whether from London or Paris I knew not, but the bar seemed to attract a new class of male customer, as it dawned on me.

She curtseyed and made off to an upstairs bar, which I learnt was newly established under her care.

I noticed that Doll's eye was on me with all the reticence of a dawn cockerel on a muck heap. She smiled, saying that Jenny had been seeking me, but was now in the country with her new employer, she knew not where.

I do not mean to trouble the reader with much detail of the royal junketing that kept the folk of Portsmouth engrossed. The King had been ill but it was given out that he was now recovered and overjoyed to be in the midst of his victorious sailors. Alas one cannot give life to descriptions of events at which one is not present.

As one familiar with Portsmouth harbour, I can only say that the oarsman-captains pulled the clumsy barge under its florid red and gold canopy with seamanlike perfection. The coxswain was Black Dick himself, and we heard the shrill pitch of the bosun's calls soar high across the water to salute the royal guests in rehearsal.

The mids and master's mates were required to vacate the gunroom mess aft to accommodate royal flunkeys and were each given an allowance for lodging ashore. There was much demand on hotels and inns to provide it, for Portsmouth was full of spectators. I fetched up in my old berth below the back stairs at the George, and it eased the demands on my pocket, being free.

Crowds poured in, and soon all the officers' rooms were taken, often by wives and families. I had to turn down the many hints from Meg to patronise her new 'retiring room', as she called the upstairs bar for gentlemen and ladies jointly, but she found frequent occasion to visit the taproom – to the great satisfaction of local patrons from the yard and round about.

In this easy setting there followed a rash of family occasions. My reconciliation with a wounded father was about to be conducted outside of the hospital walls, for he was to be discharged from Haslar, and my mother and the baby would return to Portsmouth, there to meet with Sir John, whose much-travelled coach would be at their disposal for a return to Devon. I was to book stabling and rooms at the George.

The flagship was still at the South Wall, and accommodation on board at a scarcity that still prevented our returning to the ship. Shore leave was dispensed with open-handed abandon.

The number of ships made fully sea-going was increasing daily at the Spithead, and trade was flowing down-Channel with sail o' line to escort it as before.

An air of urgency now prevailed, partly due to the fraternity of journalists having wind of French preparations to invade. The newspapers also began to report on the failure of the Channel fleet to capture the French grain convoy, in spite of the victory of June 1st.

It was ever the principal tactic of the British to attend to the enemy's battle fleet before commercial objectives.

We had done that duty irrespective of the state of the French bread basket, which Villaret had gallantly replenished. He cared naught, he said, "for the loss of a few rotten ships."

It was not until much later that we learnt the more poignant cost of the battle: the losses were heart-rending. The British had 287 men killed and 811 wounded, whilst the French suffered 1,500 killed and nearly 2,000 wounded.

I know not where the latter figures hail from, but people took to calling it the 'Glorious First of June.'

Eleanour came by post chaise, accompanied by her sister, and I hastily called for tea to be served in the reception room of the hotel to avoid the shock of my rough acquaintances of the taproom.

Ned, however, intervened on seeing that some unusual manoeuvre was under way. The old scoundrel followed me from the tap room, and hailed me and my two guests with the utmost of familiarity. I quailed when I saw the horror on their faces, much to Ned's delight and he left for more congenial waters, grinning widely. I mumbled something about ship business, ashamed at my snobbish thoughts, and ordered more refreshments. This time a dainty tray was brought by Meg, in her most expensive gown.

At her Gallic accent, my visitors' attention was riveted even more intently upon her looks and the scent she wore in profusion.

Meg stooped to whisper saucily in my ear, enquiring if monsieur wished a delicate wine to please his guests. Jewellery glistened expensively at her bosom, and as she kissed my cheek, she flashed a smile at the two sisters.

It was deliberate devilry, I was certain.

Eleanour glared at me. "Do you allow such conduct, pray?" she commenced, then changed to a pronounced shrug, as if it was of no consequence.

"Ah, that lady has saved the lives of Englishmen," I protested, while agreeing silently that it was not her concern. "Er ... including my own. Oh, she is French you know!" I added, as if it made a difference, but decided to say no more, since it might make things worse.

The ladies rose as one, and turned to ascend to their room. Ned and Meg had combined to impress the sisters of the company I kept and its total unsuitability.

In the icy silence I called a maid to show them up, and bowed politely as they departed, without a word. There was no mention of a further meeting, and I returned thankfully to the tap room. That they might return without another word troubled my mind severely.

My object was to round upon Ned for his skylark, but I learnt instead that Jemmy Bashem had left hospital to take command of a sloop in the Channel. There was little chance that his wounding on board the East Indiaman would ever be the subject of a court case, thought Ned.

Jack Parker, the gunner's mate, was recovering of his injuries too, he said.

It is time now to come to a conclusion of my family affairs, in a tale of good fortune and bad, such as might come to many a better man than I.

Hard upon the circumstances related came my mother and my baby sister, paraded by my father with just pride, for she was a jolly, bouncing infant, with the usual cargo of squalls and chuckles of her tender age. Mother handed her to a nursemaid, who whisked her away – to her cot, as I thought. I was bowing over my mother's hand, but she wanted none of that and enfolded me in her arms, as becomes the treatment of one home from the sea.

My father was less vigorous in his greeting, for he was wrapped in dressings and a sling which hoisted his arm across his chest. His back slapping of me with his undamaged arm was hearty enough, though he was still pale in his features. He took me aside and whispered that Sir John had been made chairman of the local Enclosures Commission, a right he had as Lord of the Manor and he thought I should not fear the outcome.

Doll had arranged refreshment and remained for a while to gossip, since she had performed personal services for mother after they had first spoken at Eastney barracks. She had scarcely left for the taproom than Meg came in to offer the wines for our refreshment.

Her entrance, accompanied by waiters bearing a variety of wines, produced a distinct current of interest in the military and naval people at the tables nearby. She was followed by the nursemaid in a great mob cap bearing Sophie, as they had named the baby. She was now asleep and mother took one look as she passed the wee thing for me to inspect. She looked distinctly bonny, I remarked with warmth. Indeed the small face was bright red.

When I was ready to hand little Sophie back, mother passed her on to the nursemaid as though they shared a secret which caused them such stifled merriment that they were near to explode and drop the sleeping scrap.

I was mystified and so, I sensed, were all the company.

In a sudden flash of insight, I sprang to my feet as the nursemaid turned to me and swept off the voluminous mob cap that had hidden her features.

"Jenny," I choked, "it's you, it's you at last!" I grasped her waist and held her to me, the baby between us.

She whispered my name. "Prince, you are safe!" and

her tears flowed between our cheeks. Gently she took the baby from me, and returned him to my dumbfounded mother. Everyone had fallen silent.

I saw she was exactly as in my dreams, save for her golden earrings. I fear from that moment that I ignored the room completely, leading her to the hotel's front entrance, oblivious of the astonished company. At the door we came near to colliding with Eleanour and her sister. They were hurrying in from the stair with eager expressions and dressed in the best style of Broadwell. I stood back to allow them entry but was impeded by Jenny's forward impetus and forced the sisters to one side.

There was a distinct gasp from them both and I attempted a sketchy bow. I failed sadly since Jenny clung to me, softly weeping. The rift seemed set to be final.

Jenny and I continued outside and found ourselves at the sea's edge, where wavelets swilled over the shingle in endless persistence. We sat, still entwined, Jenny abandoning the romantic speech of her nation for more ladylike English. She looked hard into my eyes, and relaxed, satisfied that there was no change between us.

It was then that Sir Josiah's assurance of her desire to settle in England came to plague my conscience with guilt. Would it be unjust of me to expect such a sacrifice of her? She, who had led a roving existence with the wild nomads of Romany, should never be tied in the shadow of her man, in spite of the oaths she had made.

In the west the evening star lit the skies above the waters of the Solent, which danced with ships' lights, as she embraced me again. I fell into a state of speechless content, conscious that the matter of her future must be resolved with her at some time.

Then, with a jolt, it came to me that I should have to

be parted from her frequently to sail with the Kings' ships, perhaps leaving her to care for my land in the deathless calm of an English village, for that was the destiny I saw.

The narrow beach was in darkness now, but a glow from the east promised the light of the rising moon that would soon illuminate our tryst among the pebbles, and it stirred us from our reveries.

I clasped her to me fiercely wanting to take her now, and Jenny responded, whispering I knew not what, so close to my throat that I felt her lips move against my neck and suddenly longed for the abandoned intimacy we had felt before.

We mumbled our utter love and my breath came as if I ran miles and miles towards her. The surf gathered strength under the moon's light, reaching for our feet and we stood up, clutching each other unsteadily and gazing at one another in awe.

"Sailorman," she said at last, "I am yours now."

She squirmed with her old fire and her eyes danced again, released from her air of solemnity.

"Pray tell me that it is proper for an Englishwoman to throw herself naked before her lover? Come, sir, come, I pray you," she pleaded with compelling impatience. "The time is ripe this minute. We must retire now to celebrate our nuptials."

THE END

GLOSSARY OF NAUTICAL TERMS

AB – a trained seaman; derived possiby from 'able-bodied'.

Admiral's coxswain – steers the admiral's personal barge.

Ahoy – a hail, official or colloquial, a greeting.

Avast – stop, cease, an order (*dimin* 'vast).

Backstay – ropes to hold masts against pressure from aft (standing rigging).

Banyan – fig tree; slang for party or raid ashore.

Barky - pet name for any sailing ship.

Blackstrap – dark wine of South Mediterranean, issued in lieu of rum ration.

Boatswain (bosun) – seaman warrant officer, responsible for maintenance of sails, anchors, ropes – not boats – and daily work, piping the watches to work etc.

Bosun's call – a silver whistle used by the bosun.

Bounty – civic payment to volunteers for Navy.

Braced – square sail moved by braces from yardarms

Brails – lines for drawing fore and aft sails up to gaff prior to furling, similar to clew lines on square sail.

Bullocks – nickname for the marines.

Bumboat – small boat trading to ships in harbour.

Cable – one tenth nautical mile/200 yds. Large rope.

Capstan – vertical winch for winding up anchors.

Carronade – a light-weight cannon firing a large bore for 'battering' at short range.

Cathead – a projection on bows for anchor work.

Clew up – to draw up foot of sail by clew lines (see 'brails').

Commodore – a senior captain temporarily in charge of other vessels at sea.

GLOSSARY OF NAUTICAL TERMS

Corsair – pirate, or his ship, origin in Mediterranean, oared.

Corvette – small flush deck warship with one tier of guns, fast, sometimes Bermuda-rigged ie the fore and aft sail leading edge close to mast full length.

Counter – ship's overhanging stern.

Cuddy – a small den or cabin, esp. in boats.

Cully – term for unhandy, inexpert mate.

Cutting out party – raid to re-take boats, or prisoners.

Dogs/Dog watch – a two-hour watch; first 1600-1800, last 1800-2000 to rotate daily watches.

Dolphin – structure in harbour for mooring to.

Double-tides – overtime, extra watches (paid).

Fairlead – ships' fitments to turn a rope's direction, often through blocks, aimed to ease its running with the least friction.

Fathom – linear measurement six feet, used to show depths on older charts, sounding lines etc.

Falls – hauling part of a tackle, the part handled.

Field rank – British army term for ranks above captain.

Fifth – slang for fifth lieutenant, usually additional to normal complement of four in a ship of the line.

First rate ship – ship of line, 100 guns or more.

Fo'c'stlemen – waisters, after guard – ship's company tending fore, main and mizzen masts.

Frigate – fifth or sixth rate ship of 20 – 38 guns and 160 – 250 complement of crew. Not in line of battle.

Futtock shrouds – short ropes below tops to stay the topmast rigging, made fast to lower masts.

Gaff cutter – one-mast vessel, the fore and aft mainsail carried on a 'gaff,' a hoisted yard, peak at top.

Gig – captain's boat of narrow, smooth-planked build, eight-oared or more.

GLOSSARY OF NAUTICAL TERMS

Grappling iron – hook on line thrown to attach to or grapple another, ship, jetty, etc.
Gunnel (gunwale) – top plank of a boat's side.
Hand – to furl sail, also to shorten or reduce.
Halliards – line or purchase for hoisting objects.
Hawse – piercing of bow for anchor cable. Also Space ahead on seabed for anchoring.
Hoy – small sailing coaster for passengers and goods.
Jacob's ladder – rope ladder, wood-runged.
Jollies - nickname for the marines.
Jollyboat – ship's work boat, 6 or more oared.
Ketch – small vessel, two-masted fore and aft sails. The mizzen is small and set before tiller head.
Langridge – metal scrap fired from cannons, grape.
Lee – opposite to 'weather,' sheltered side.
Lobscouse – sailor's stew of meat, vegetables, bran.
Long nine – a long-barrelled gun for 9lb roundshots. Often used in ships' bows.
Longshoreman – dockside worker, not a seaman.
Lubber hole – confined space next to mast used by 'new men' to reach top. Topmen climb under futtock shrouds and over top's outside rim.
Lugger – vessel,fore and aft rigged, four-sided lugsails.
Man-o-war's-man – veteran retained in peace.
Mizzen peak – upper point of hoistable sloping yard fore and aft on a mizzen mast (the aftermost mast).
Needles – seamark, white rocks on the west of the Isle of Wight.
On a split yarn – poised for action, in the balance.
Petty officer – non-commissioned, equivalent to an army sergeant.
Prize – a ship or property captured in war. 'Condemned' as such by Admiralty Court, its value is showed by all

present at the capture on a scale according to seniority of rank – 'prize money.' This practice was abolished after World War II.

Ratlins – rope rungs across shrouds for climbing aloft.

Royals – square sails next above topgallants.

Running rigging – this is hauled or let-go, to move the sails, yards etc, often through the blocks of tackles to gain more purchase.

Salutes at sea – made by bosun's call, junior ship to senior, who replies twice followed by junior ship.

Schooner – a sailing ship with two or more masts.

Scrimshaw – sailors' hobby of making plaques, using shells, whalebone etc. Usually for sale.

Seine net – fishing net, disposed on floats to circle shoals of fish, closed by two ships. Also by men fishing from beach.

Sheet in – order to haul sheets aft.

Sheets – ropes to lower corners of sq sail, or after corner of fore and aft sail.

Shrouds – rope stays to hold masts at each side.

Side – name of salute on bosun's call for captains and admirals commanding at sea, arriving or leaving ship.

Sloop – a sailing ship with one mast.

Slop chit – purser's voucher for goods taken on charge.

Splice the main brace – slang, order for extra rum.

Squadron – a fleet is divided into Van (white), Centre (red) and Rear (blue) squadrons distinguished by ensigns above, and further into 'divisions'.

Standing rigging – fixed ropes to stay masts etc.

Starboard gangway – reserved for senior officers.

Sternsheets/foresheets – inner fabric at stern and bow of ship's boat.

Strike colours – to hand down national flag as token of a ship's surrender. Hostilities ceased.

Tacking – to alter course, head thro' wind on zigzag track to make headway to windward.

Taff rail – the rail on the back of a ship.

Thwart – oarsman's seat at 90° to line of boat.

Top – platforms atop lower mastheads, used by topmen tending sail and marksmen in action.

Topgallant – square sail next above topsail.

Trick – sailor's period of duty on lookout, wheel etc.

Truck – circular piece atop mast, holds halliards.

Veer – to pay out into sea, eg a log-line, a tow.

Wear – to turn a square rigger ship, stern to wind.

Weather – side or direction from which wind blows.

White ensign – worn by ships of Van squadron in 1790s. Now worn by entire Navy.

APPENDIX 1

Battle of the Glorious First of June
28th May to 1st June 1794

THE BRITISH LINE OF BATTLE

VAN

	guns
Caesar	80
Bellerophon	74
Leviathan	74
Russell	74
Royal Sovereign*	100
Marlborough	74
Defence	74
Impregnable	98
Tremendous	74
Barfleur	90
Invincible	74
Culloden	74

CENTRE

	guns
Gibraltar	80
Queen Charlotte*	100
Brunswick	74
Valiant	74
Orion	74
Queen	98

REAR

Ramillies	74
Alfred	74
Montagu	74
Royal George*	100
Majestic	74
Glory	98
Thunderer	74

* VAN   Adml. Thomas Graves – Royal Sovereign
  CENTRE Adml. Earl Howe, C-in-C – Queen Charlotte
  REAR   Adml. Sir Alexander Hood – Royal George

APPENDIX 2

Battle of the Glorious First of June
28th May to 1st June 1794

THE FRENCH LINE OF BATTLE

	guns		guns
Trajan	74	Montagne*	110
Eole	74	Jacobin	80
Amerique	74	Achille	74
Temmeraire	74	Vengeur de Peuple	74
Terrible*	110	Patriote	74
Impetueux	74	Northumberland	74
Mucius	74	Entreprenante	74
Tourville	74	Jemappes	74
Gasparin	74	Neptune	74
Convention	74	Pelletier	74
Trente-et-Un Mai	74	Republicaine*	110
Tyrannicide	74	Sans Pareil	80
Juste	80	Scipion	80

* Flag officers:
  RA Francois-Josef Bouvet, Second in Command – Le Terrible
  RA Louis-Thomas Villaret Joyeuse, C-in-C – Le Montagne
  RA Josef-Marie Neilly - La Republicaine.

ABOUT THE AUTHOR

John Francis was born in 1923 in Shrewsbury and spent his early years in Church Stretton, Shropshire, a small market town surrounded by the beautiful hills, grouse moors and craggy valleys leading to the Welsh border. Here in the local school he met two teachers who inspired their pupils with tales of the sea and nautical ballads. One old song particularly impressed him with the lines:

> 'and we jolly sailor boys were up and up aloft
> with the landlubbers lying down below...'

He attended grammar school in Shrewsbury and at 18, during the war with Germany, Francis joined the Navy. Gaining a commission as a sub lieutenant RNVR, he served in the operations against Hitler's Western flank, in Normandy. He joined the battles of the Atlantic convoys, subsequently moving to the Mediterranean in a minesweeper and later a destroyer. He was promoted to Lieutenant RN, staying in the Navy until 1953 when his term of service ended.

Ashore, Francis joined the Ministry of Defence as a civil servant, where he stayed until retirement. He remained a dedicated seaman, being offered a berth in the sailing ship *Royalist*, and later became mate in the topgallant schooner *Youth of Oman*. He founded a sail training school, based at Falmouth, of which he is extremely proud – his pupils have since populated the seas worldwide.

In recent years, he has written a number of poems and short stories, all with a nautical theme, some of which have been published. He now lives in the Cotswolds with his wife Anne, where he writes and enjoys the pleasures of the countryside.

As with every sailor, there comes a time to 'swallow the hook'. But when a soft northerly blows, Francis fancies he can hear the old shanties, sung by the sweet tones of young voices and recalls those two dear schoolmarms with grateful affection.

ACKNOWLEDGEMENTS

Special thanks are due to a number of people for their contribution to the writing, editing, and publishing of this book. They are (in alphabetical order) Elissa Collier, Anne Francis, Joanna Gonet, Marianne Hinton and Alex Murray – as well as the members of the Cotswold Writers Group.